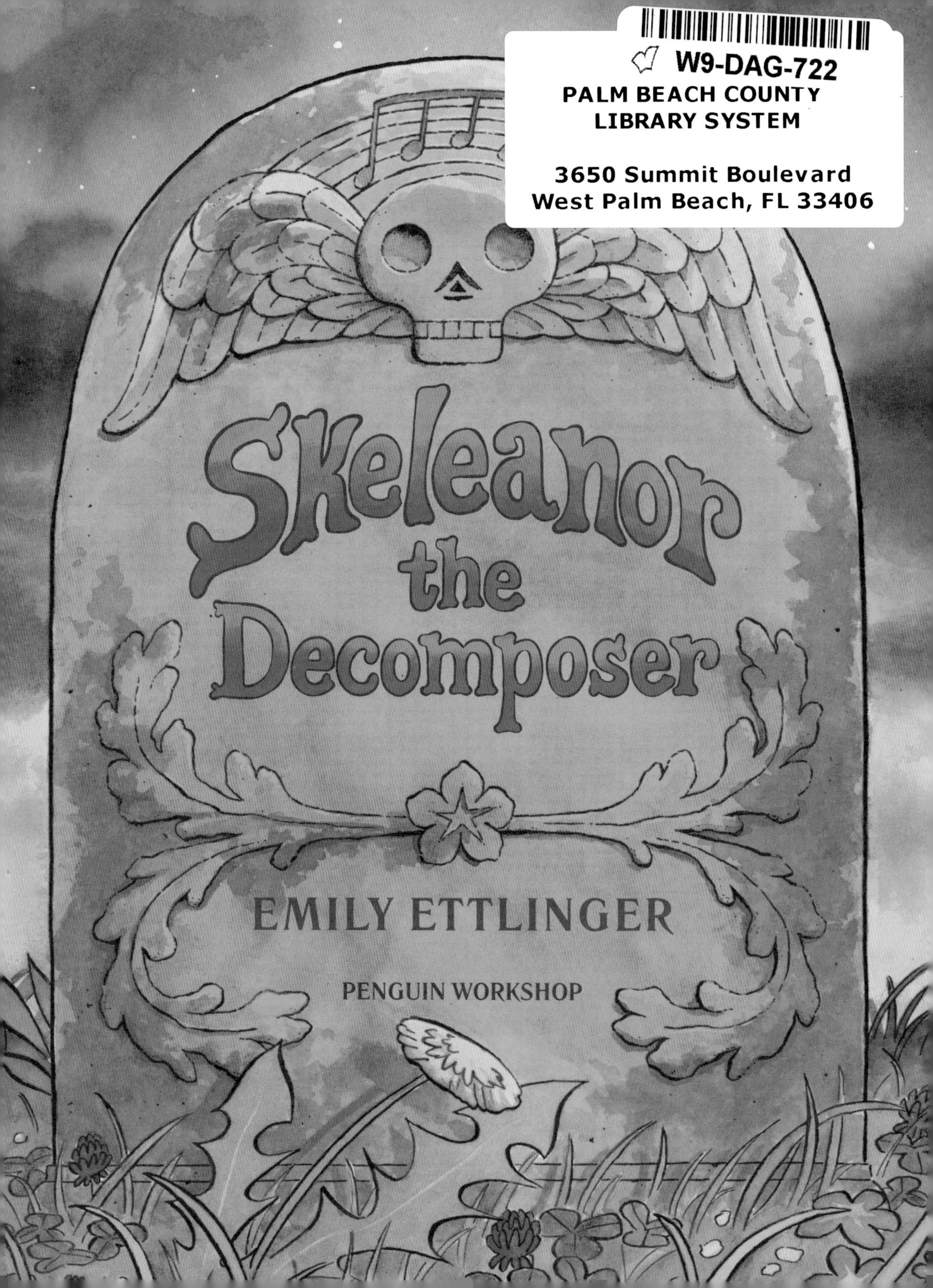
Skeleanor the Decomposer
EMILY ETTLINGER
PENGUIN WORKSHOP

To Mara—
We'll meet again.

PENGUIN WORKSHOP
An imprint of Penguin Random House LLC, New York

First published in the United States of America by Penguin Workshop,
an imprint of Penguin Random House LLC, New York, 2023

Visit us online at penguinrandomhouse.com.

Library of Congress Cataloging-in-Publication Data is available.

Manufactured in China

ISBN 9780593519448   10 9 8 7 6 5 4 3 2 1 HH

Design by Jay Emmanuel
Lettering by Tess Stone

CHAPTER 1

SKELEANOR AND THE GREAT AUDITION

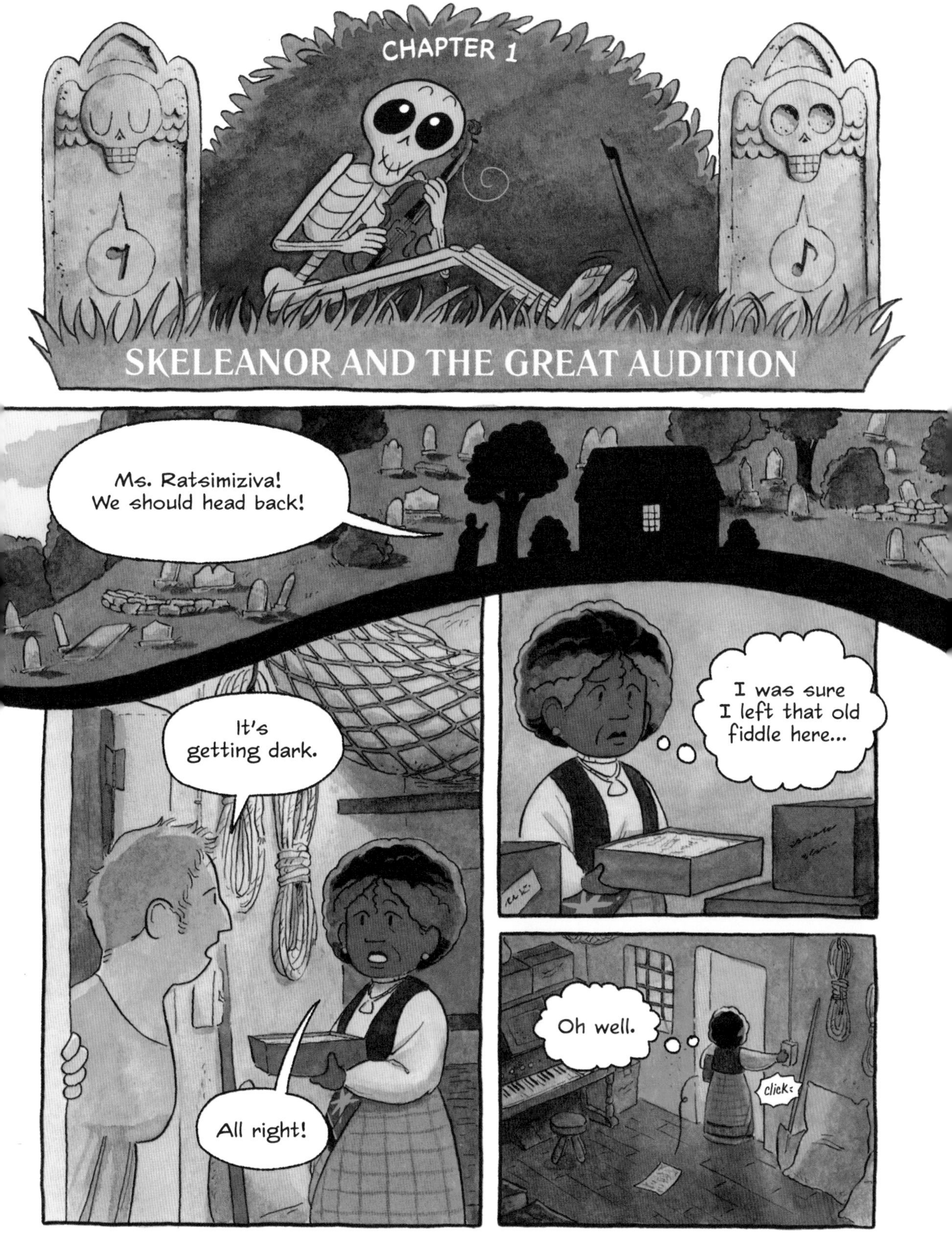
Ms. Ratsimiziva! We should head back!
It's getting dark.
All right!
I was sure I left that old fiddle here...
Oh well.
click

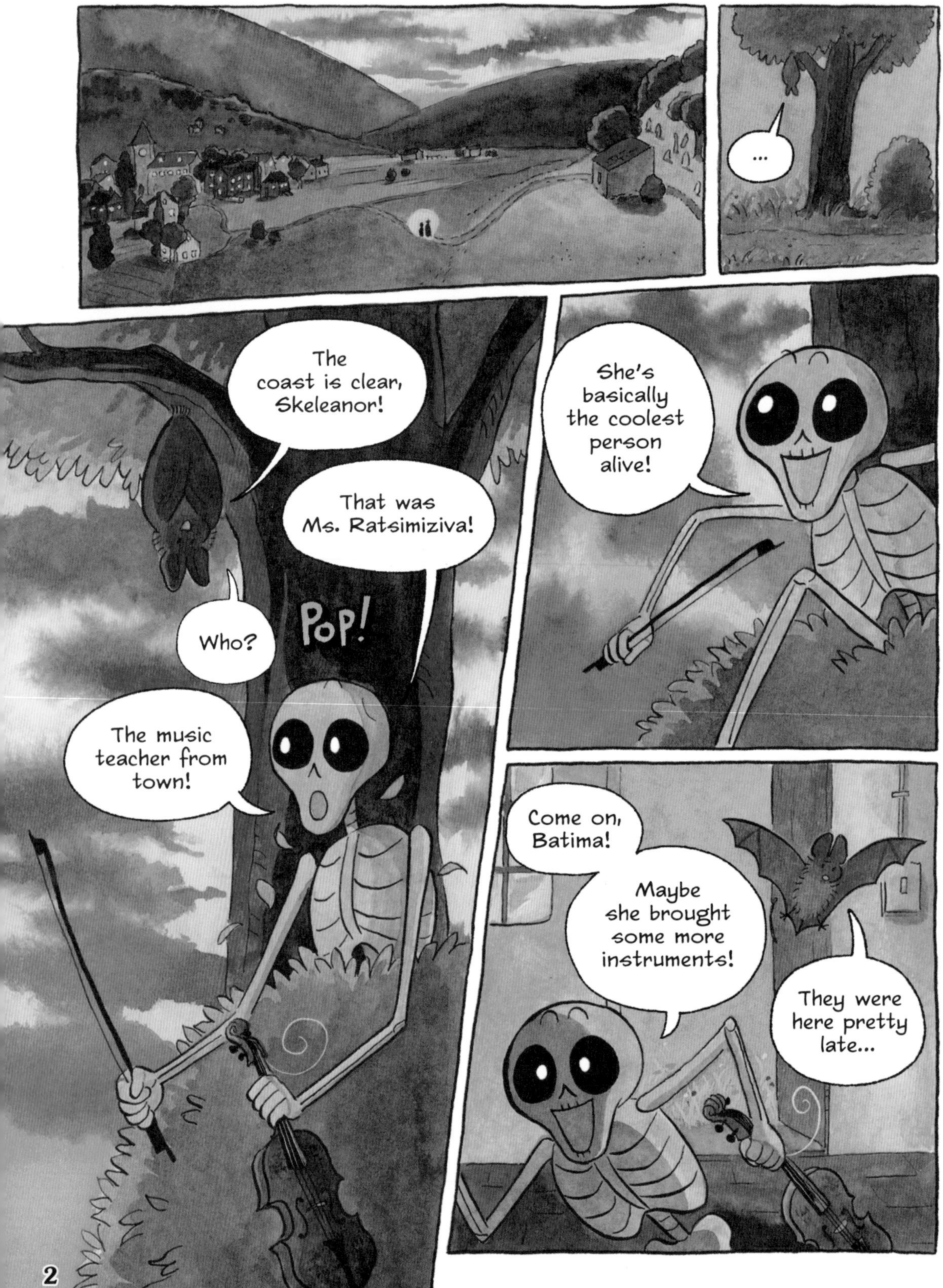
...
The coast is clear, Skeleanor!
That was Ms. Ratsimiziva!
Who?
POP!
The music teacher from town!
She's basically the coolest person alive!
Come on, Batima!
Maybe she brought some more instruments!
They were here pretty late...

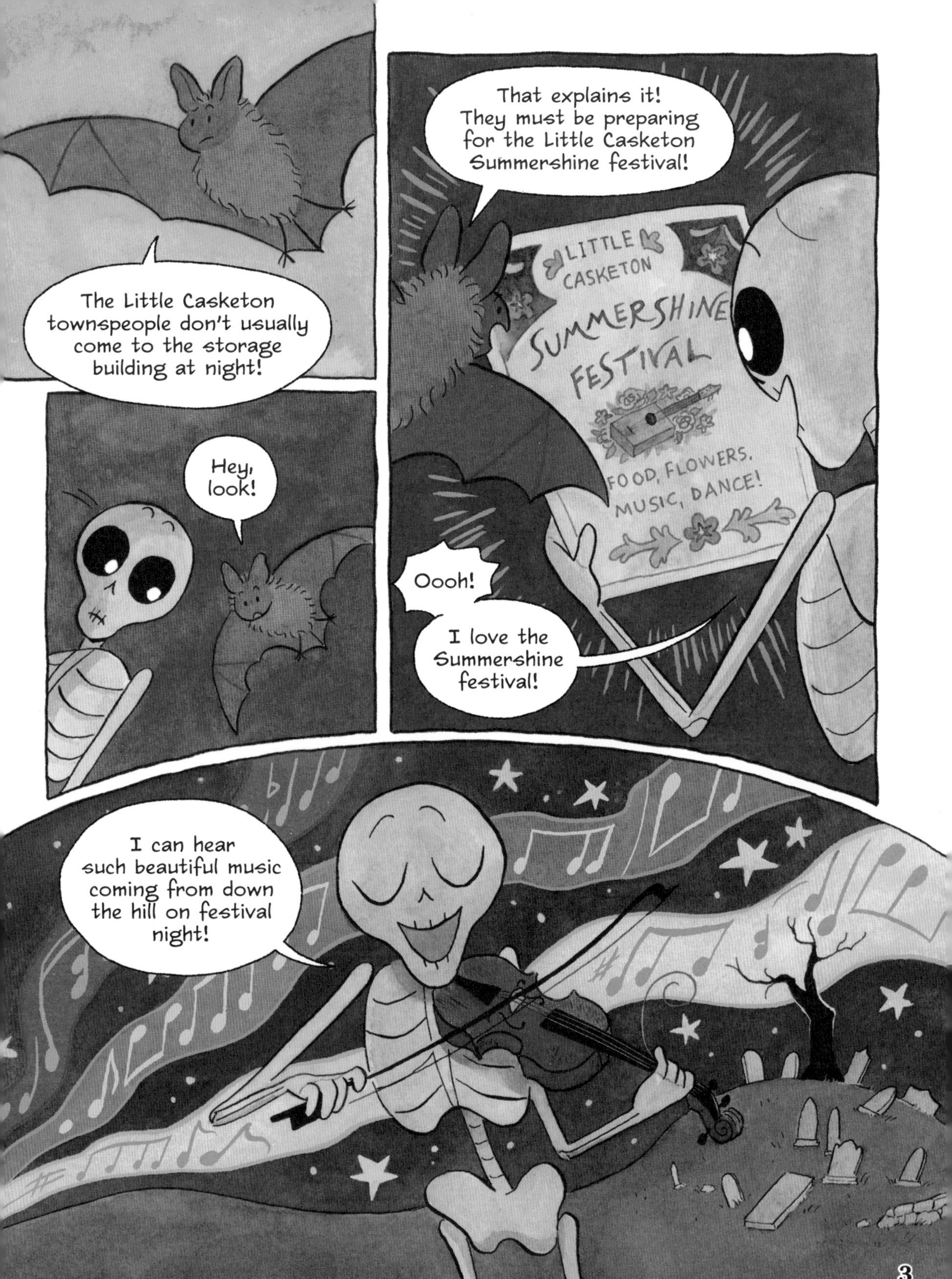
The Little Casketon townspeople don't usually come to the storage building at night!
That explains it! They must be preparing for the Little Casketon Summershine festival!
LITTLE CASKETON SUMMERSHINE FESTIVAL
FOOD, FLOWERS. MUSIC, DANCE!
Hey, look!
Oooh!
I love the Summershine festival!
I can hear such beautiful music coming from down the hill on festival night!

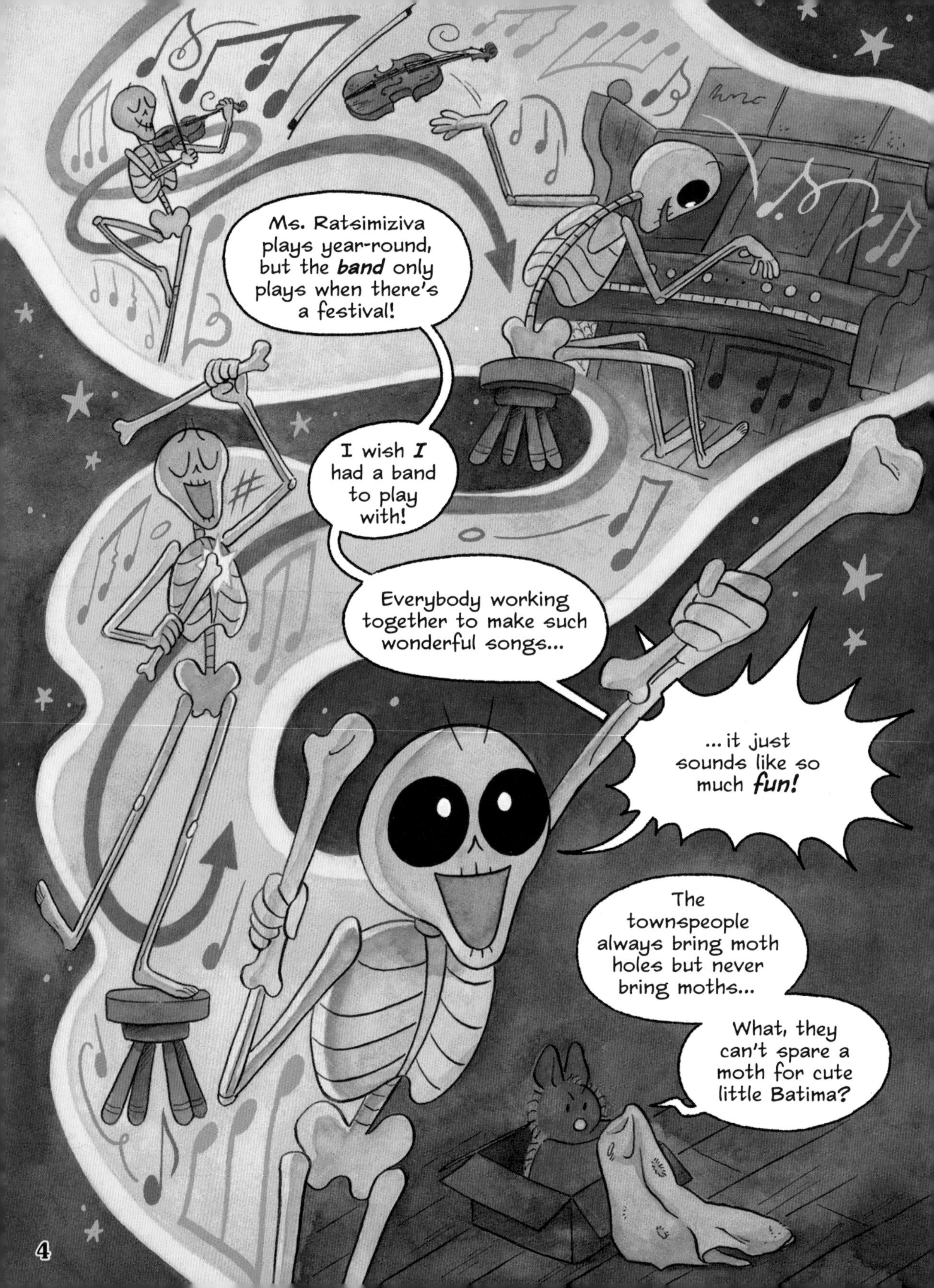
Ms. Ratsimiziva plays year-round, but the *band* only plays when there's a festival!
I wish *I* had a band to play with!
Everybody working together to make such wonderful songs...
...it just sounds like so much *fun!*
The townspeople always bring moth holes but never bring moths...
What, they can't spare a moth for cute little Batima?

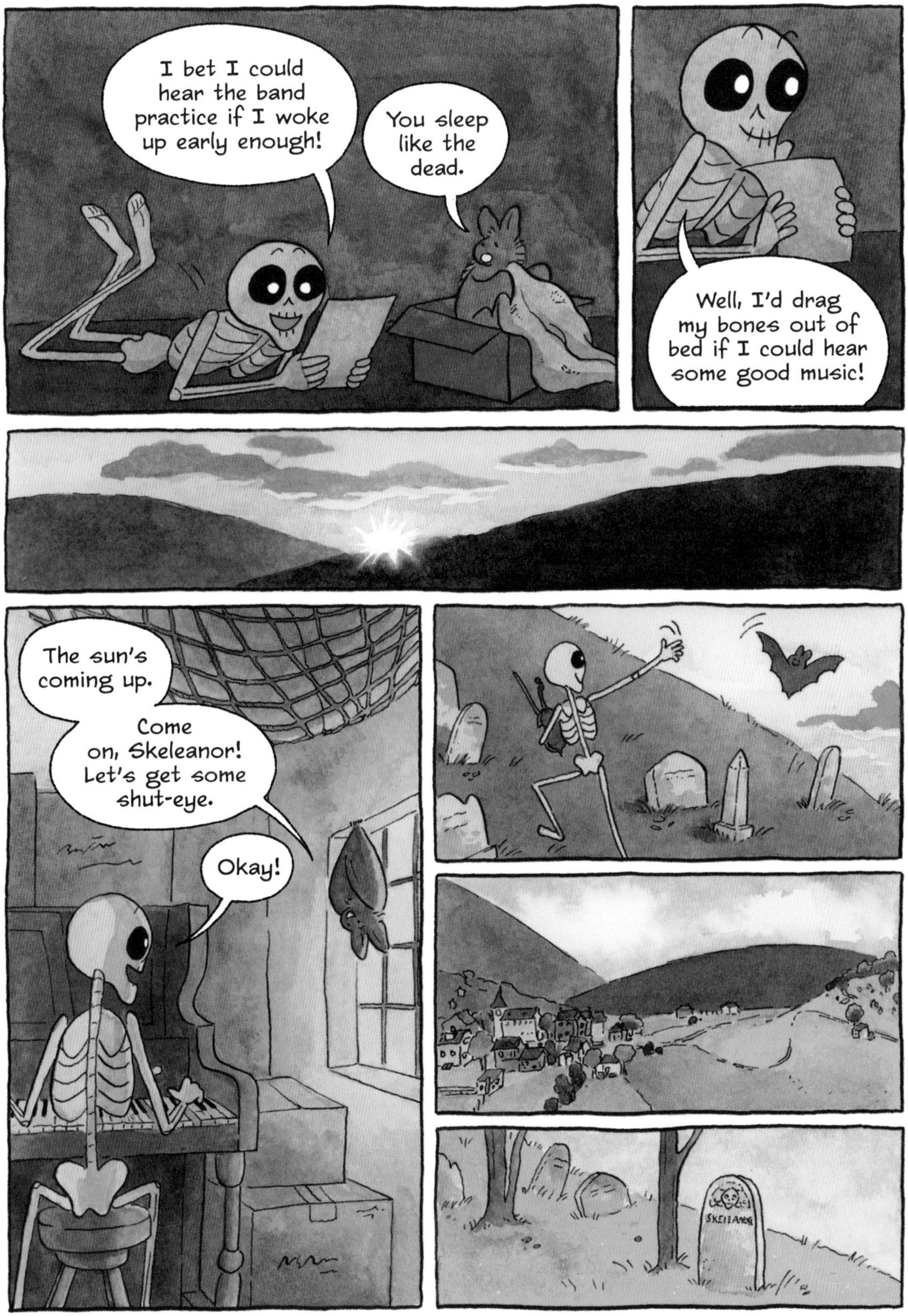
I bet I could hear the band practice if I woke up early enough!
You sleep like the dead.
Well, I'd drag my bones out of bed if I could hear some good music!
The sun's coming up.
Come on, Skeleanor! Let's get some shut-eye.
Okay!

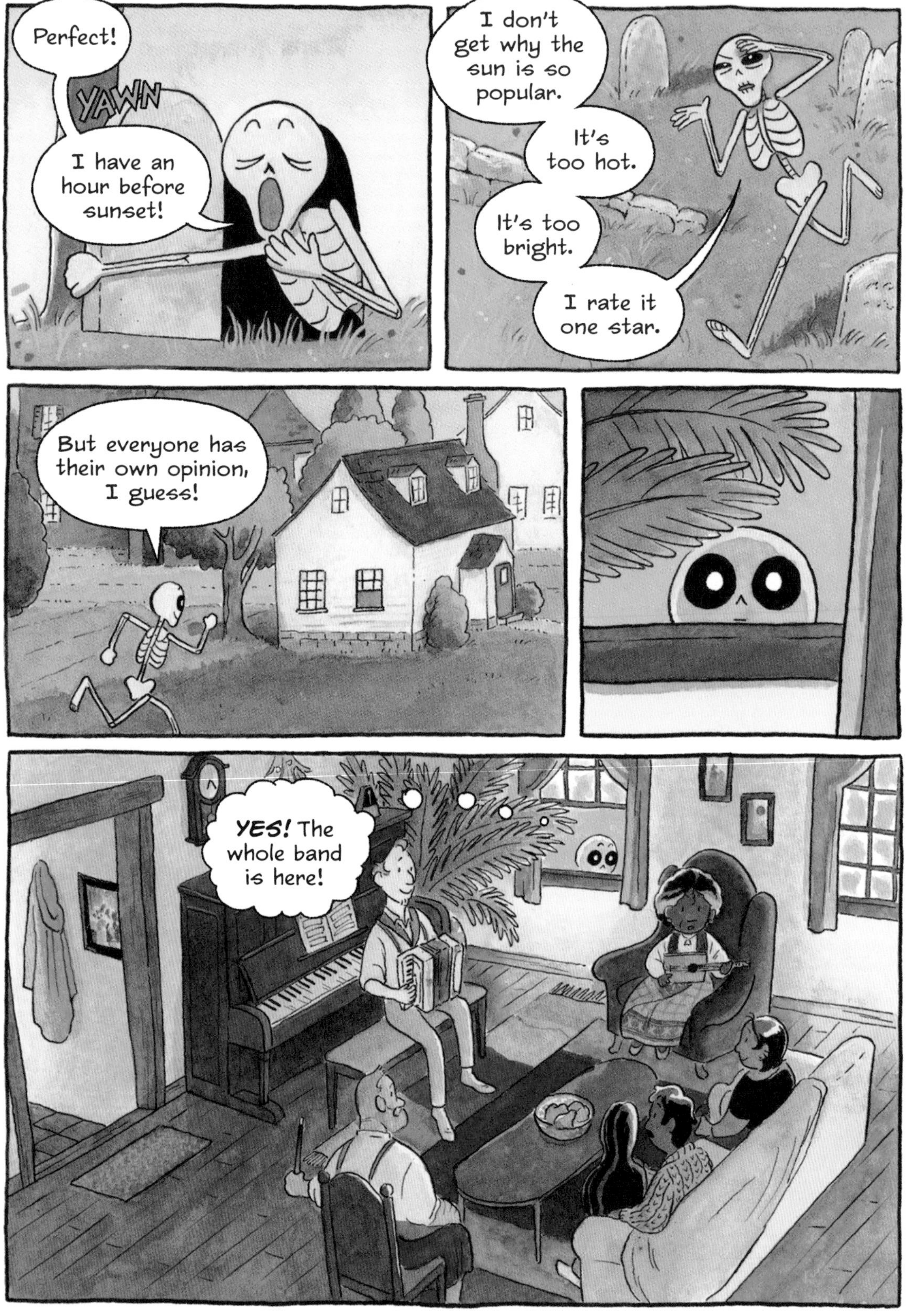
Perfect!
YAWN
I have an hour before sunset!
I don't get why the sun is so popular.
It's too hot.
It's too bright.
I rate it one star.
But everyone has their own opinion, I guess!
YES! The whole band is here!

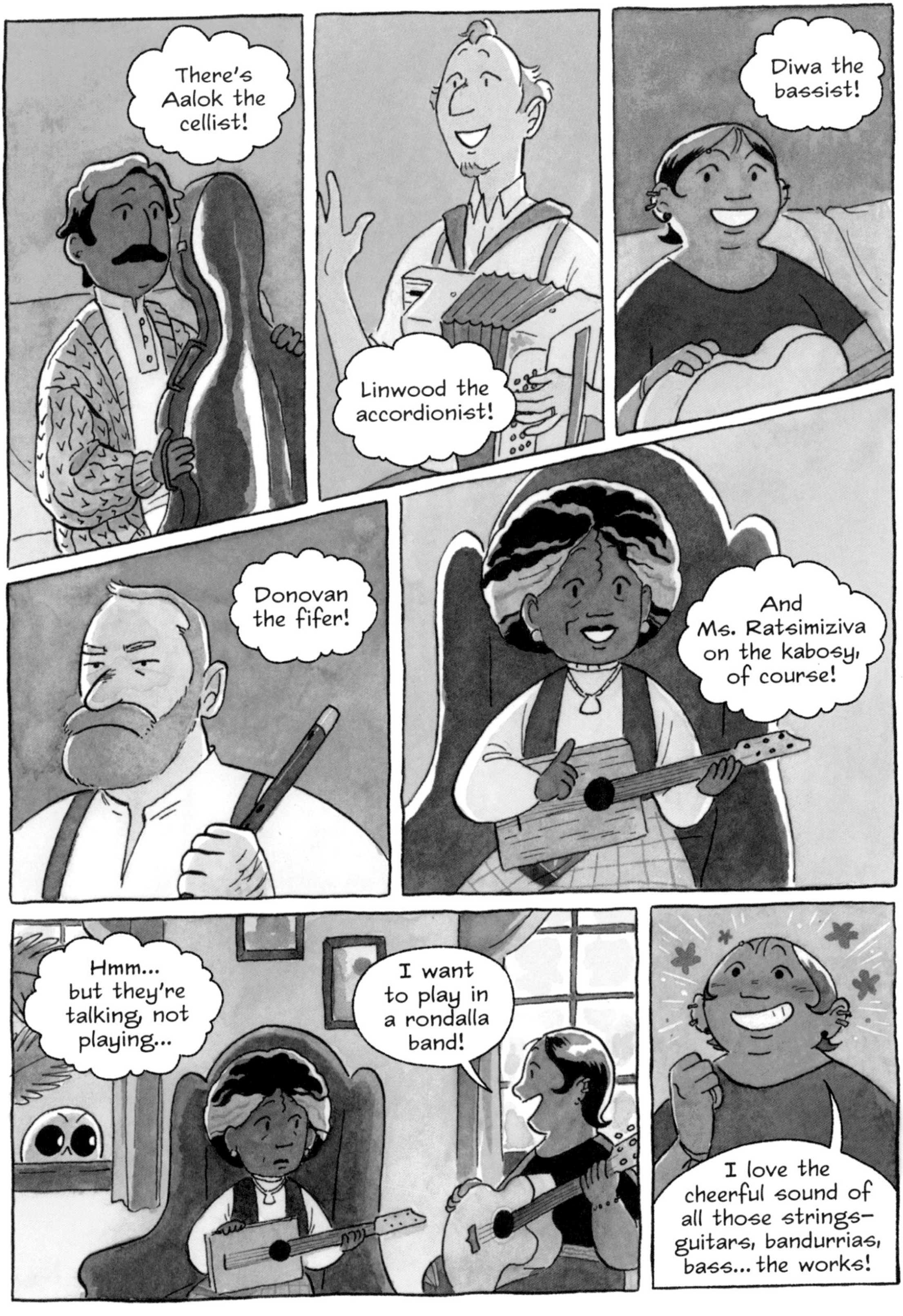
There's Aalok the cellist!
Linwood the accordionist!
Diwa the bassist!
Donovan the fifer!
And Ms. Ratsimiziva on the kabosy, of course!
Hmm... but they're talking, not playing...
I want to play in a rondalla band!
I love the cheerful sound of all those strings— guitars, bandurrias, bass... the works!

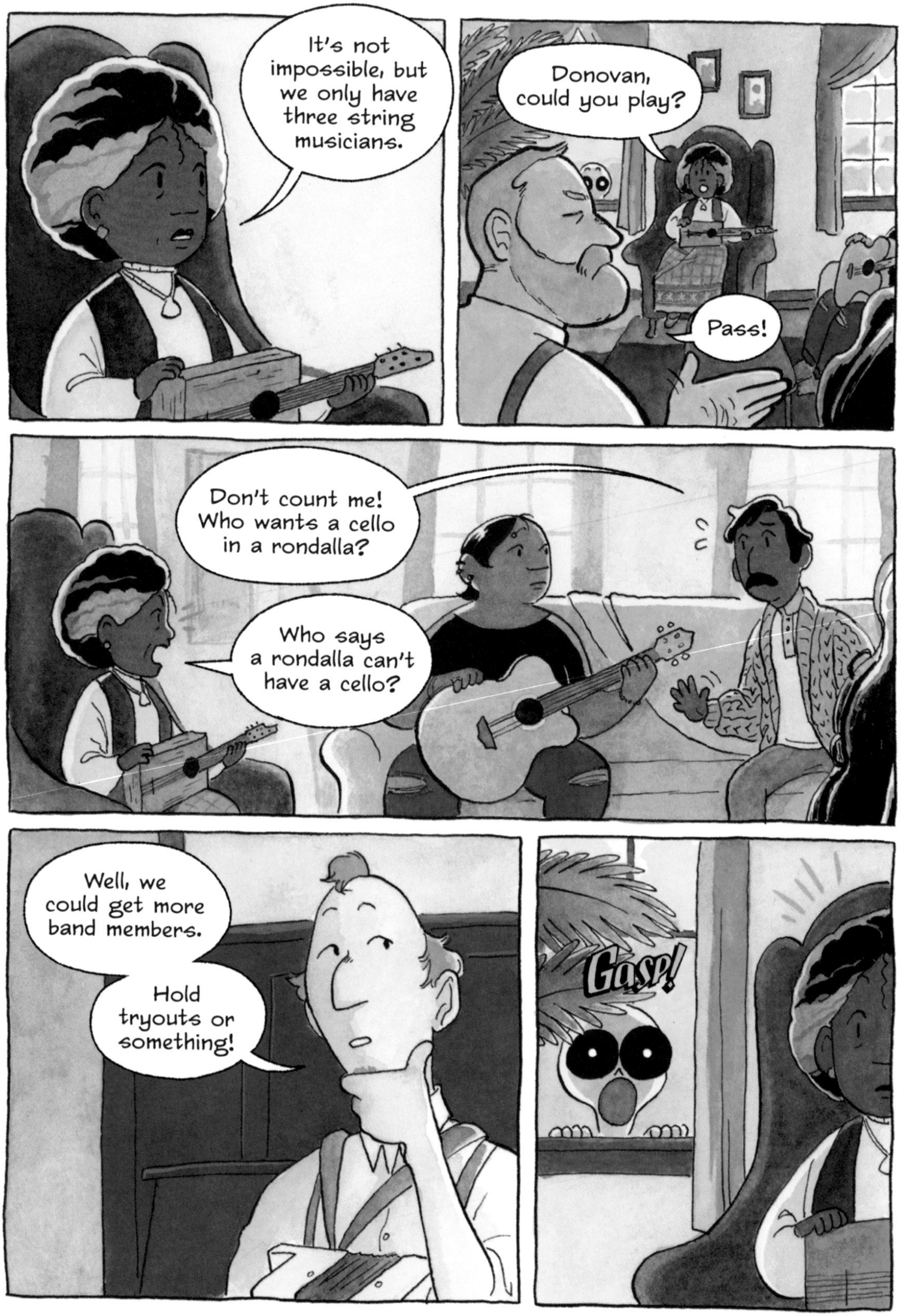

It's not impossible, but we only have three string musicians.
Donovan, could you play?
Pass!
Don't count me! Who wants a cello in a rondalla?
Who says a rondalla can't have a cello?
Well, we could get more band members.
Hold tryouts or something!
Gasp!

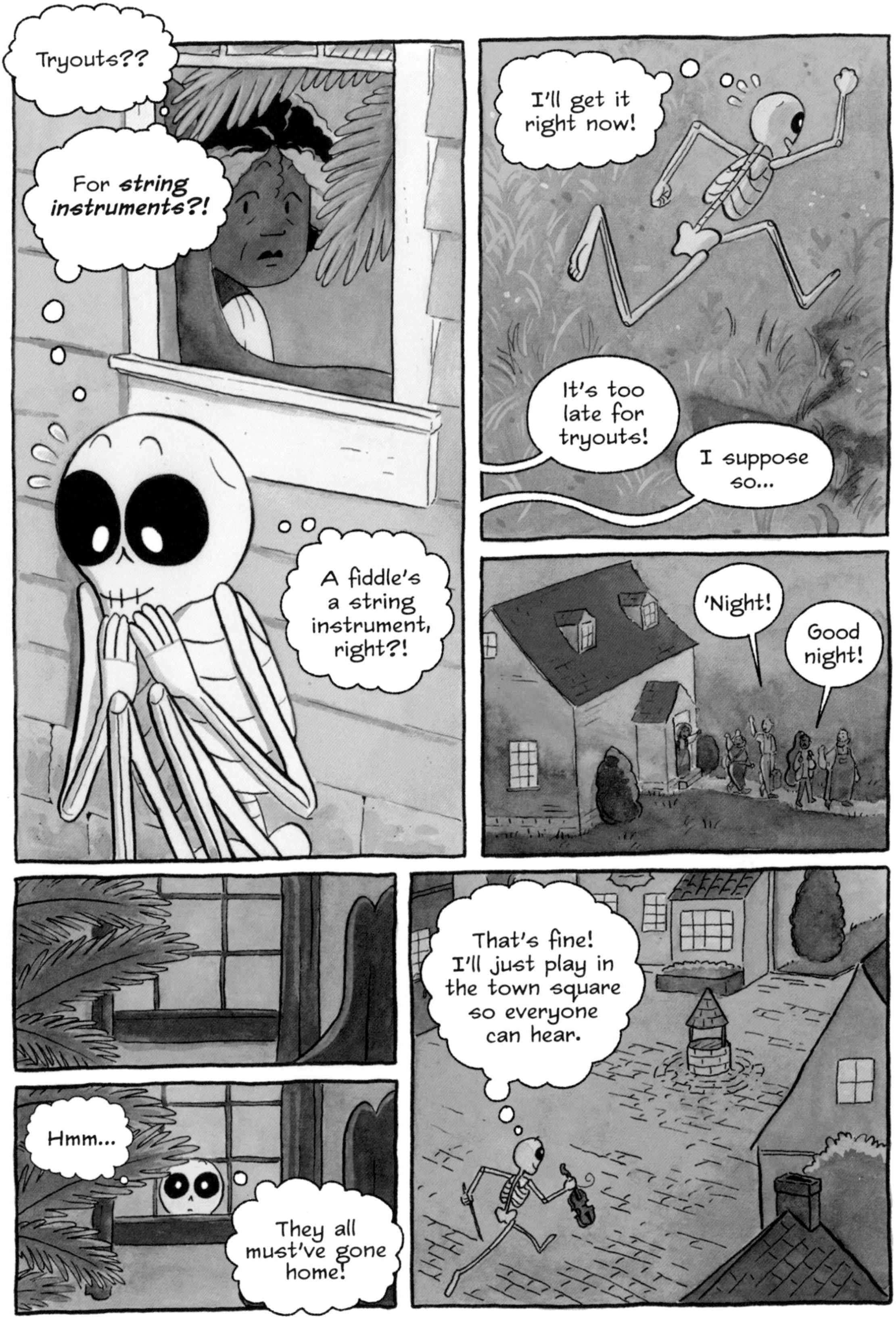
Tryouts??
For *string instruments?!*
A fiddle's a string instrument, right?!
I'll get it right now!
It's too late for tryouts!
I suppose so...
'Night!
Good night!
Hmm...
They all must've gone home!
That's fine! I'll just play in the town square so everyone can hear.

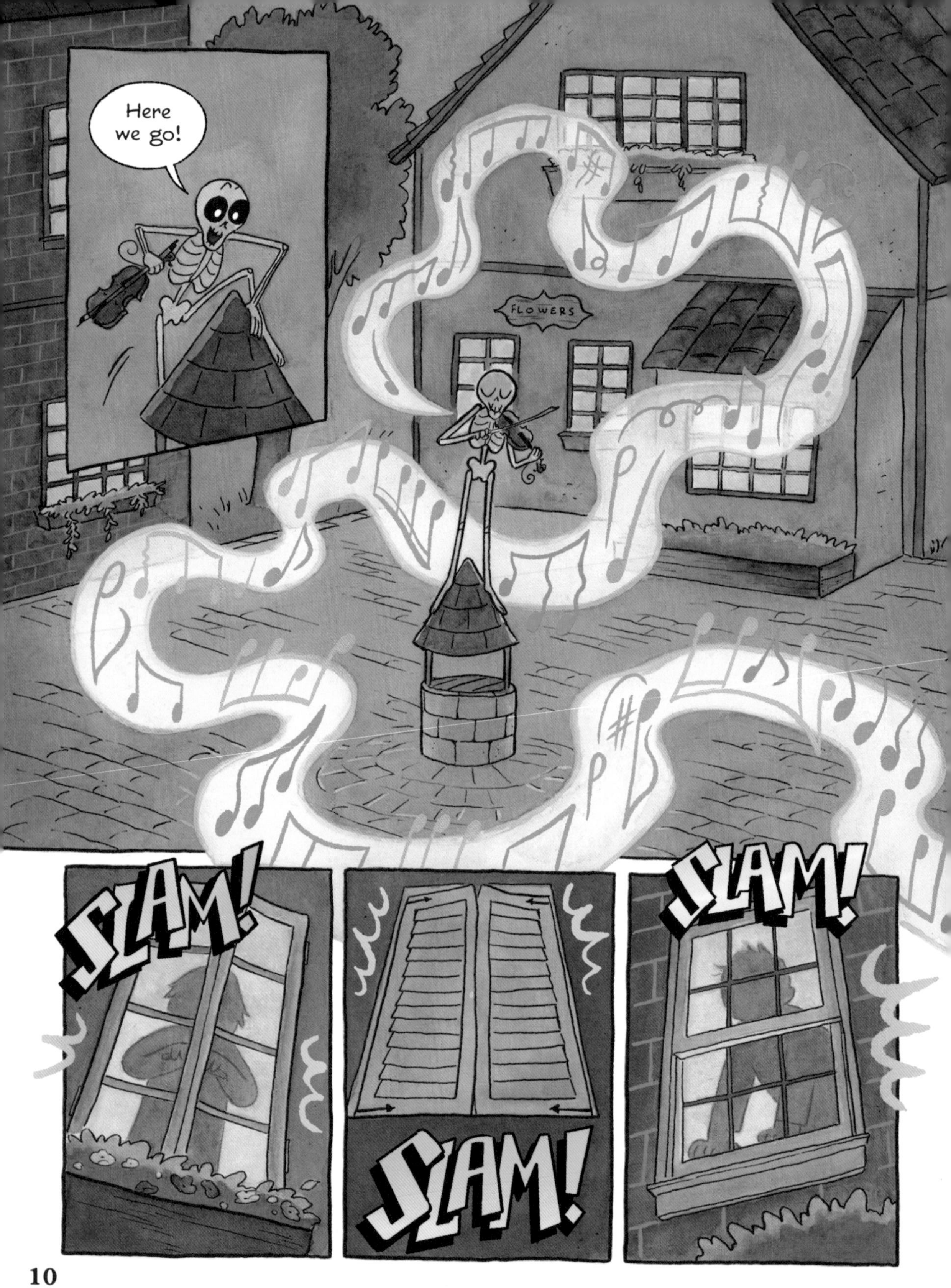
Here we go!
FLOWERS
SLAM!
SLAM!
SLAM!

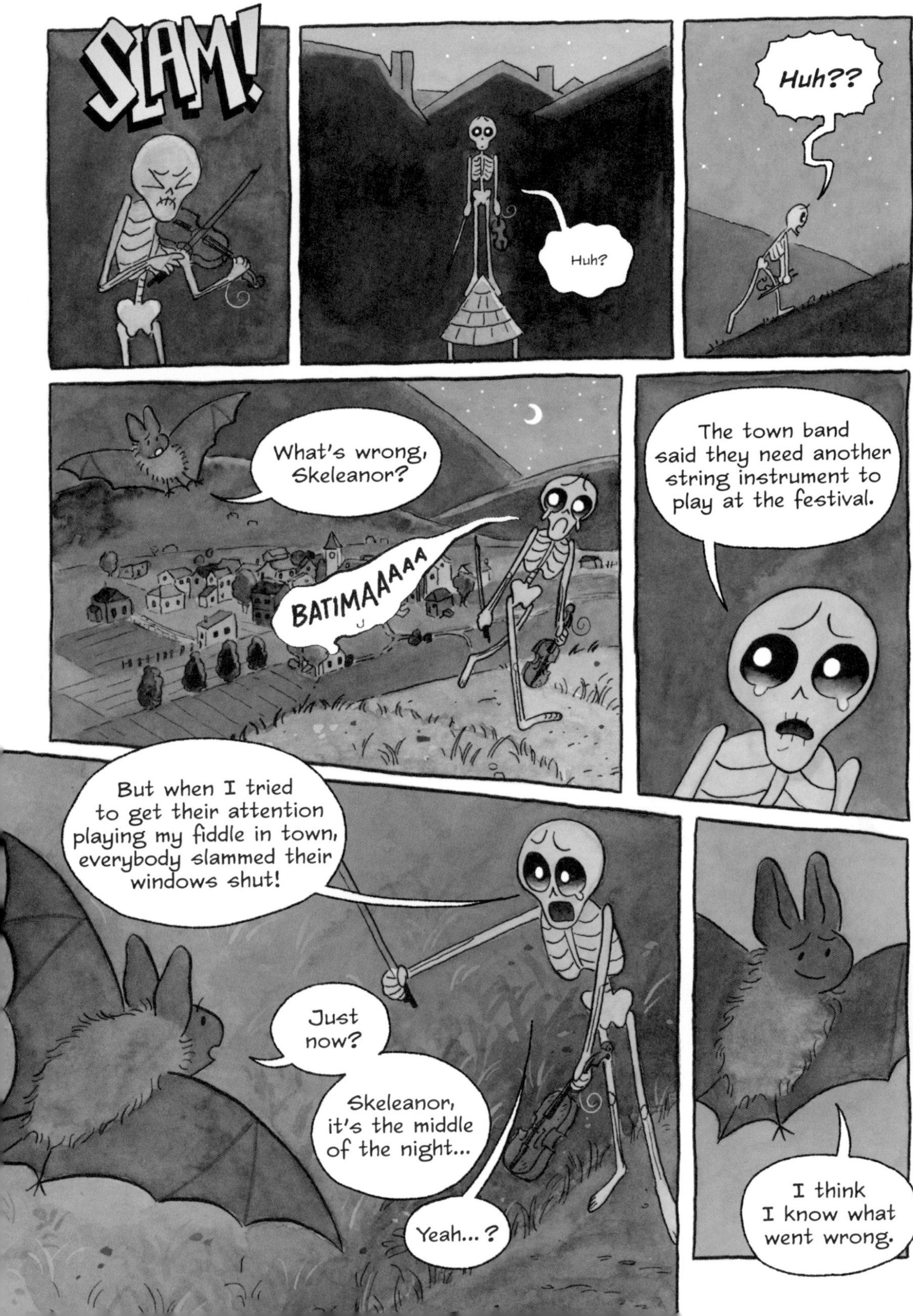
SLAM!
Huh?
Huh??
What's wrong, Skeleanor?
BATIMAAAAA
The town band said they need another string instrument to play at the festival.
But when I tried to get their attention playing my fiddle in town, everybody slammed their windows shut!
Just now?
Skeleanor, it's the middle of the night...
Yeah...?
I think I know what went wrong.

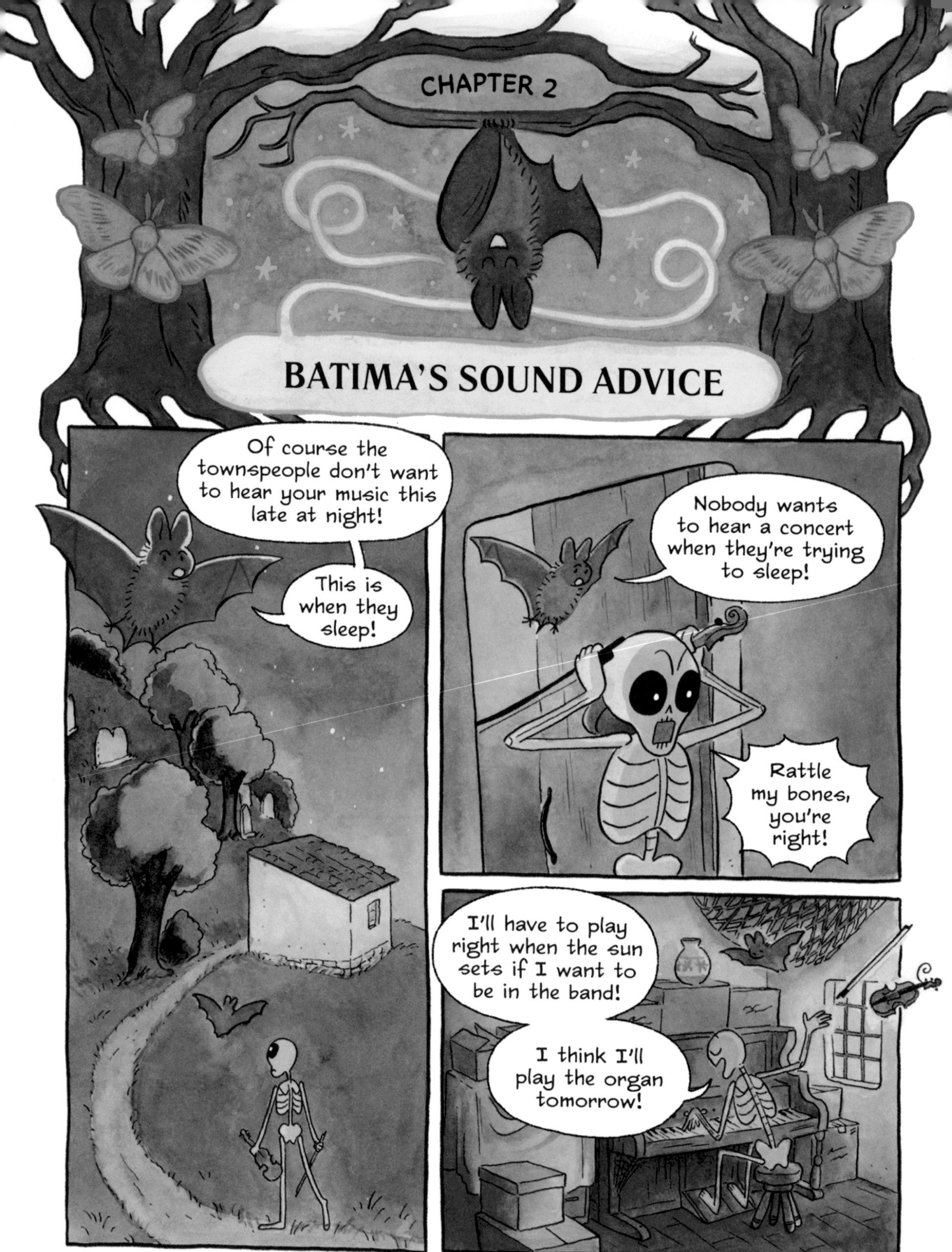
CHAPTER 2
BATIMA'S SOUND ADVICE
Of course the townspeople don't want to hear your music this late at night!
This is when they sleep!
Nobody wants to hear a concert when they're trying to sleep!
Rattle my bones, you're right!
I'll have to play right when the sun sets if I want to be in the band!
I think I'll play the organ tomorrow!

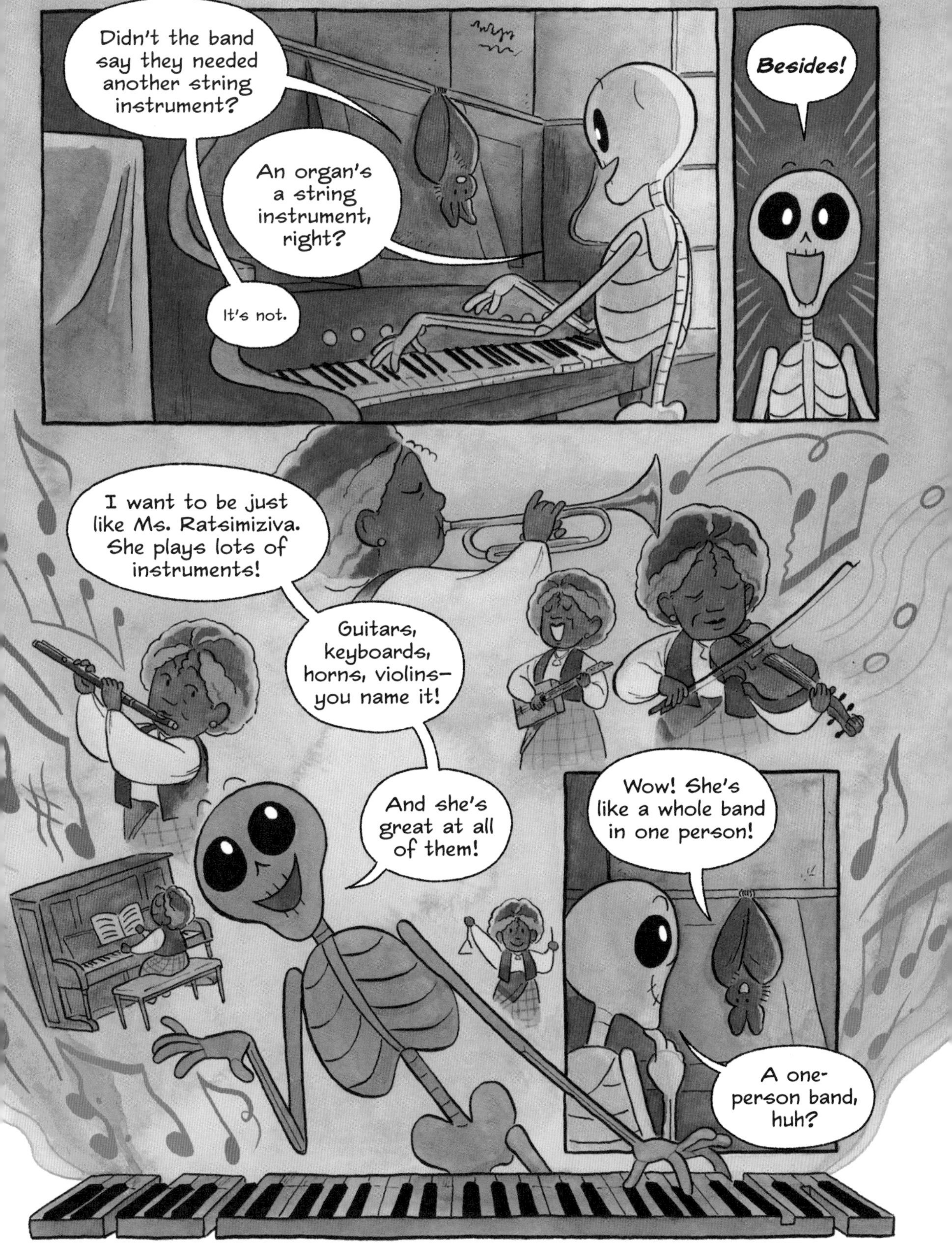
Didn't the band say they needed another string instrument?
An organ's a string instrument, right?
It's not.
Besides!
I want to be just like Ms. Ratsimiziva. She plays lots of instruments!
Guitars, keyboards, horns, violins– you name it!
And she's great at all of them!
Wow! She's like a whole band in one person!
A one-person band, huh?

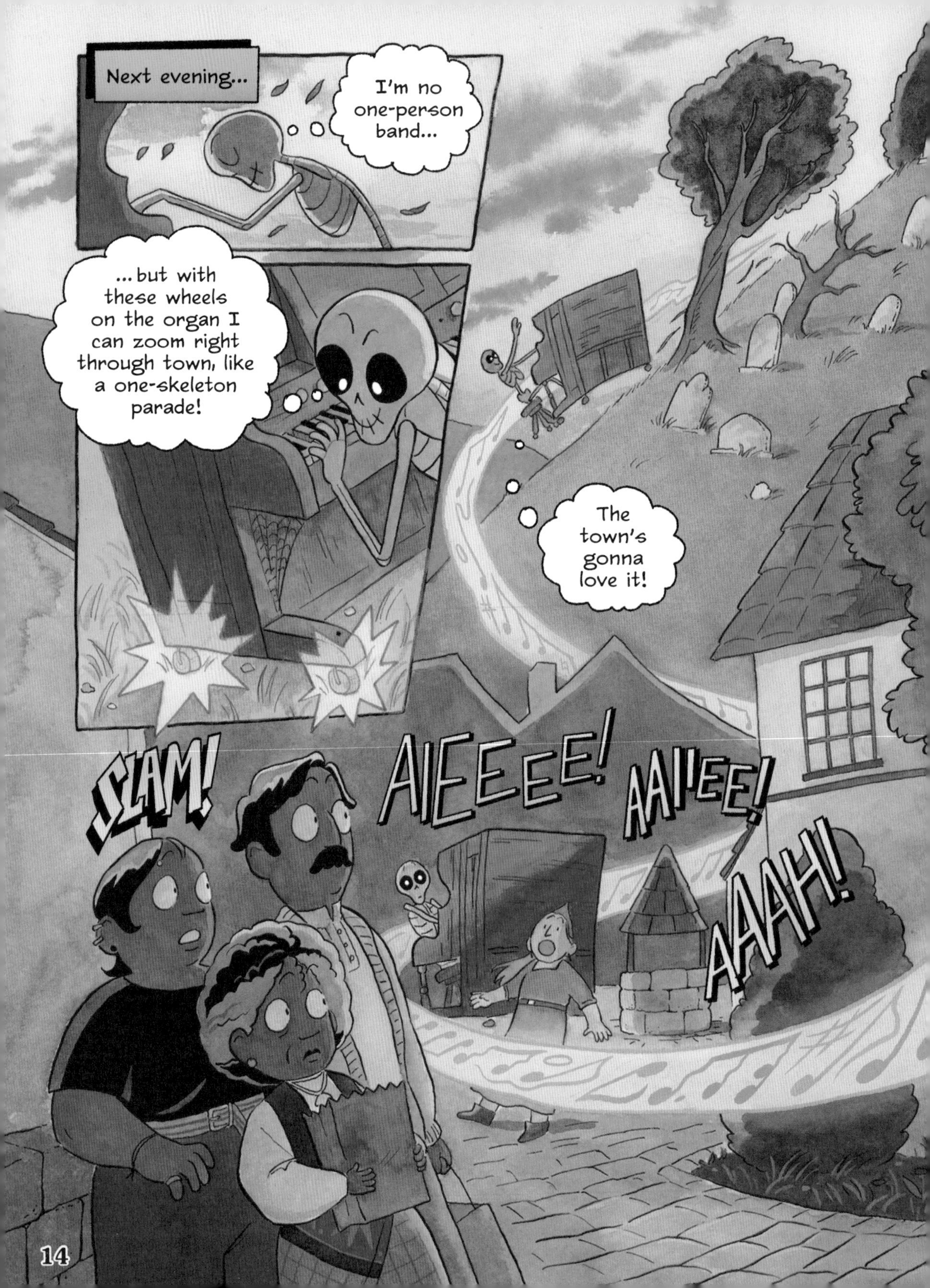
Next evening...
I'm no one-person band...
...but with these wheels on the organ I can zoom right through town, like a one-skeleton parade!
The town's gonna love it!
SLAM!
AIEEEEE!
AAIEEE!
AAAH!

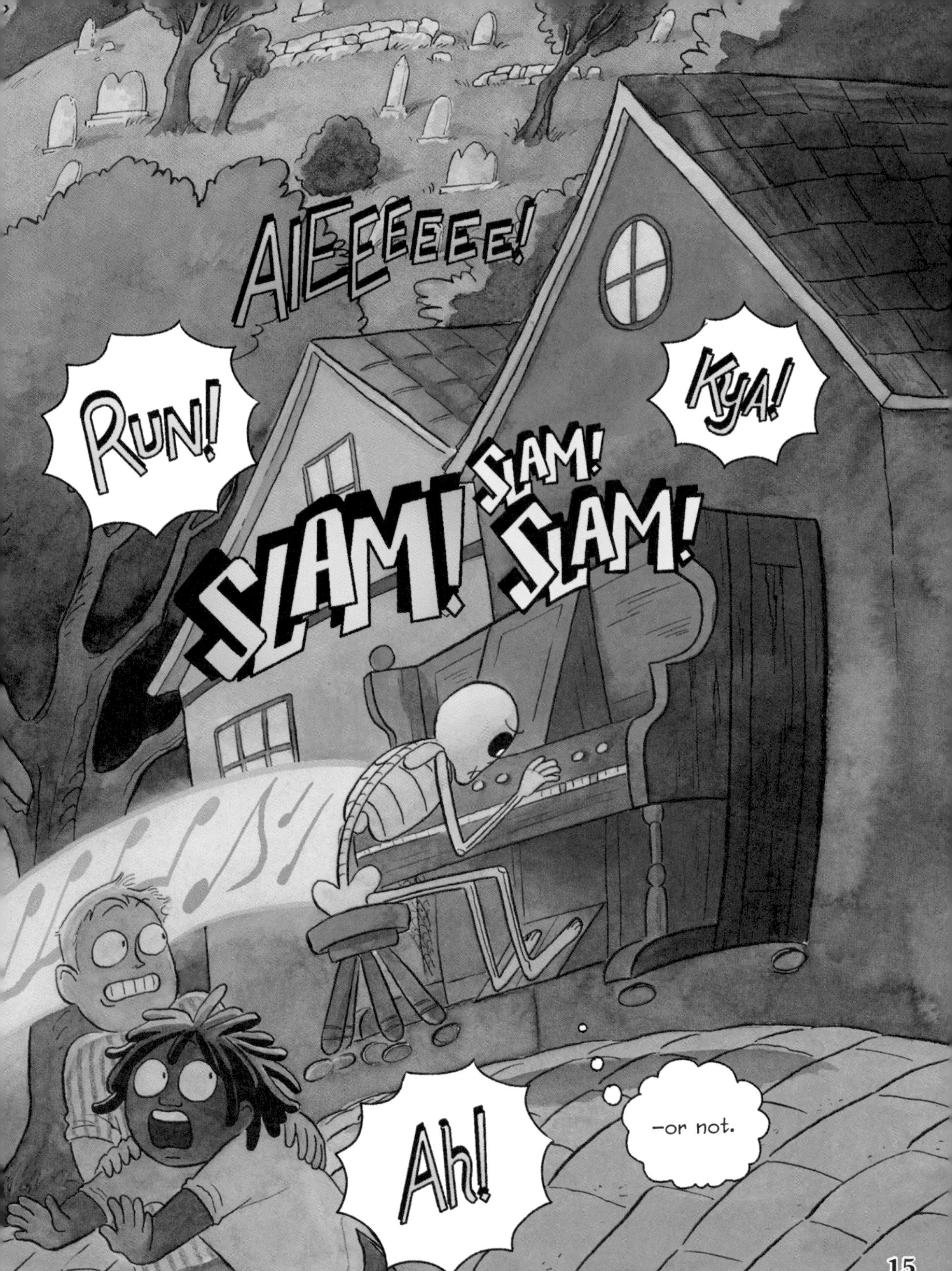
AIEEEEEEE!
RUN!
KYA!
SLAM! SLAM! SLAM! SLAM!
Ah!
–or not.

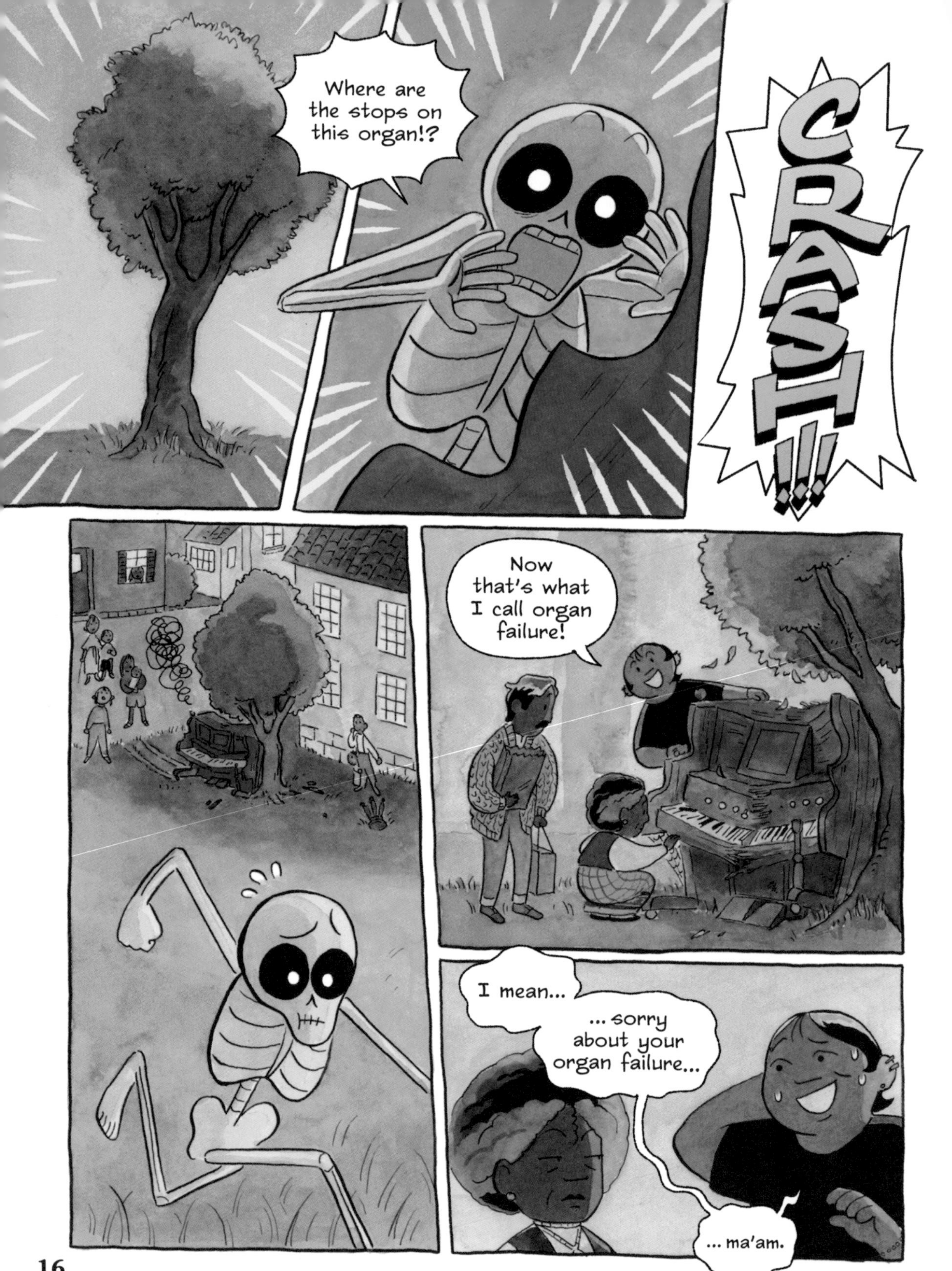

Where are the stops on this organ!?
CRASH!!!
Now that's what I call organ failure!
I mean...
... sorry about your organ failure...
... ma'am.

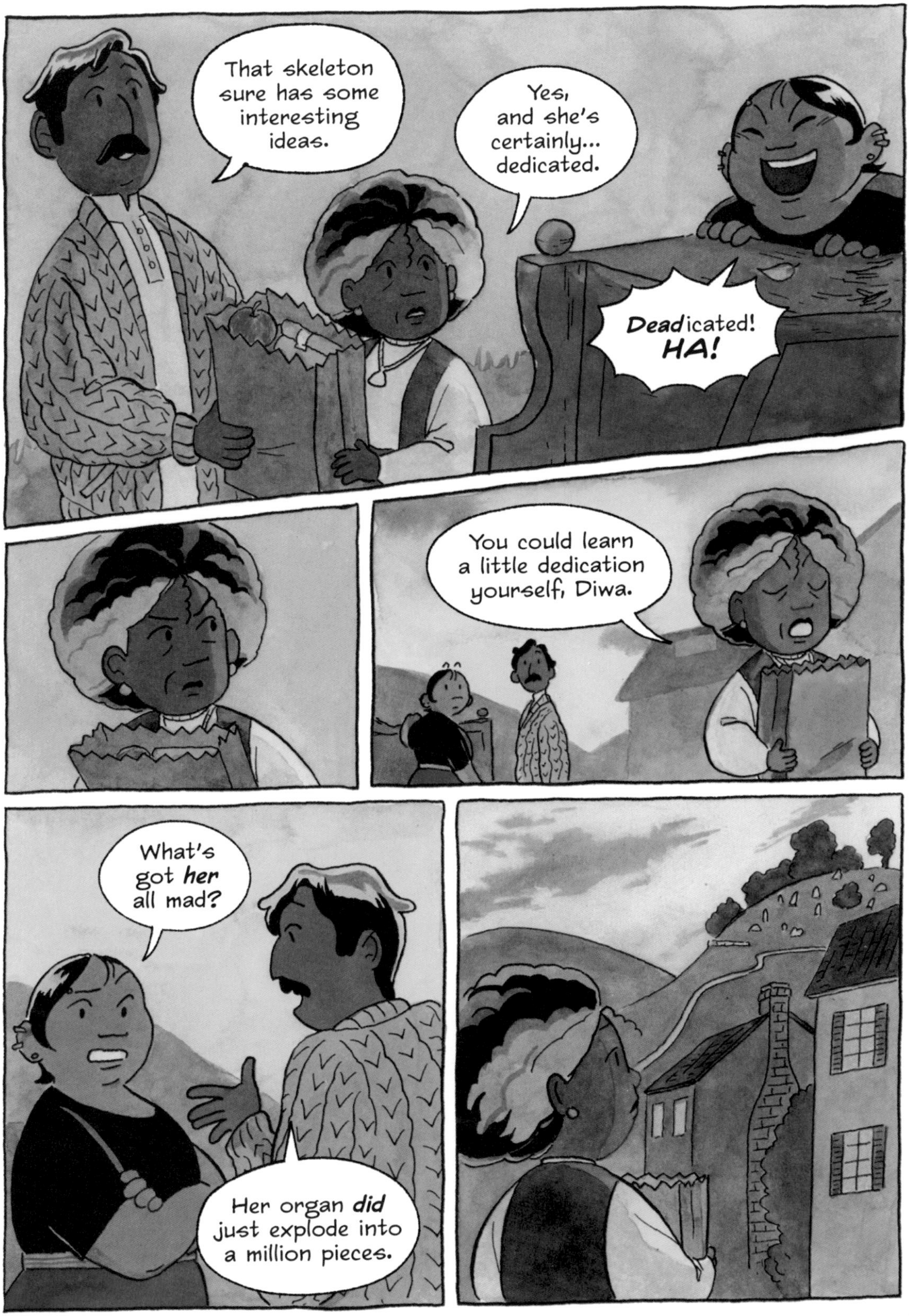
That skeleton sure has some interesting ideas.
Yes, and she's certainly... dedicated.
*Dead*icated! *HA!*
You could learn a little dedication yourself, Diwa.
What's got *her* all mad?
Her organ *did* just explode into a million pieces.

Hmm...

This grasshopper I just caught would be delicious fresh...

TUESDAY WEDNESDAY THURSDAY FRII

But if I wait to eat the june bug it'll get stale.

HHHH
HHHRR
R
R
RRMMMM
mmmmaaybee

I'll just toss it...

BATIMA!!

Agh!

I'M SORRY! I WON'T WASTE FOOD!

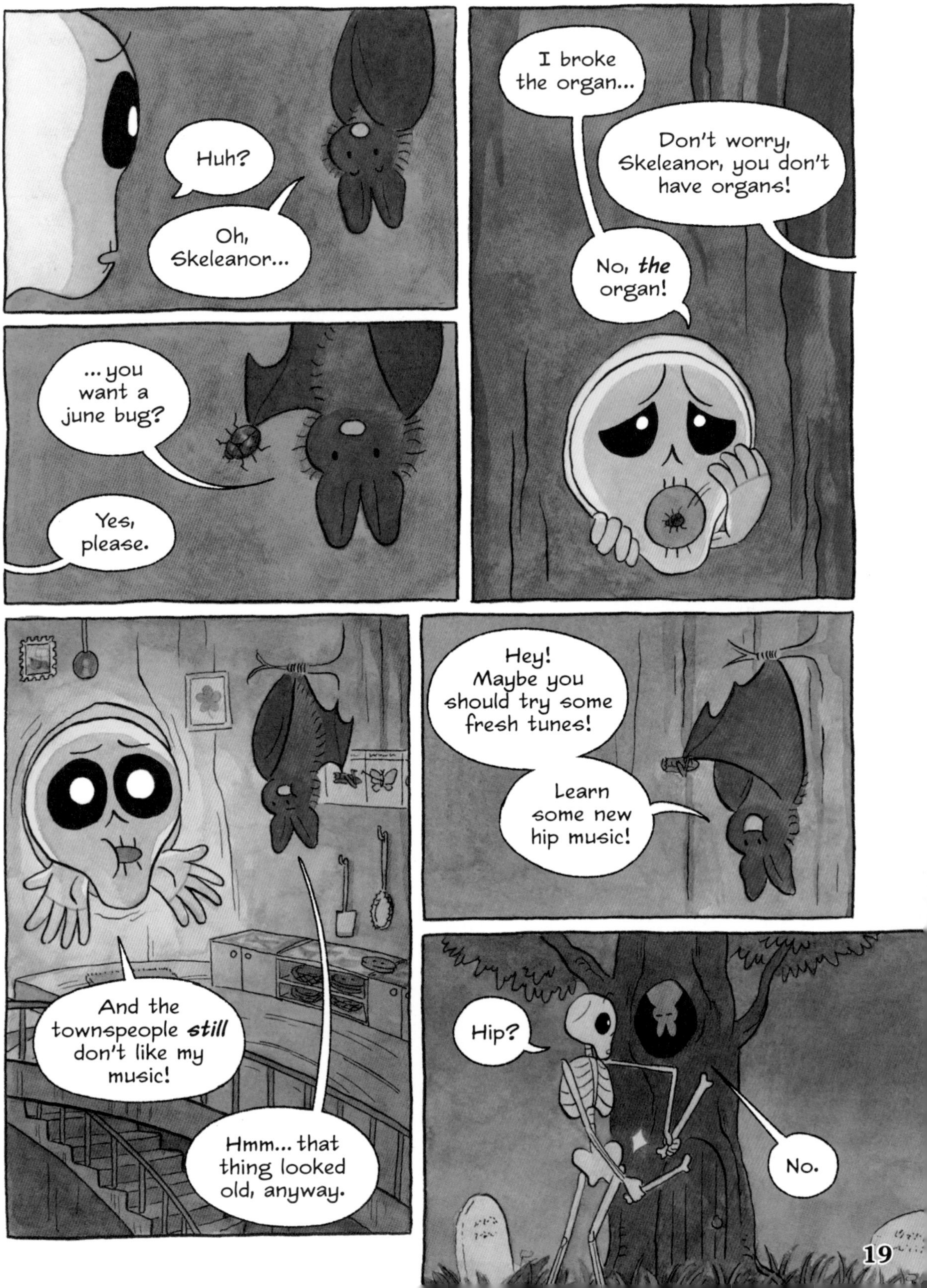
Huh?
Oh, Skeleanor...
...you want a june bug?
Yes, please.
I broke the organ...
Don't worry, Skeleanor, you don't have organs!
No, *the* organ!
And the townspeople *still* don't like my music!
Hmm... that thing looked old, anyway.
Hey! Maybe you should try some fresh tunes!
Learn some new hip music!
Hip?
No.

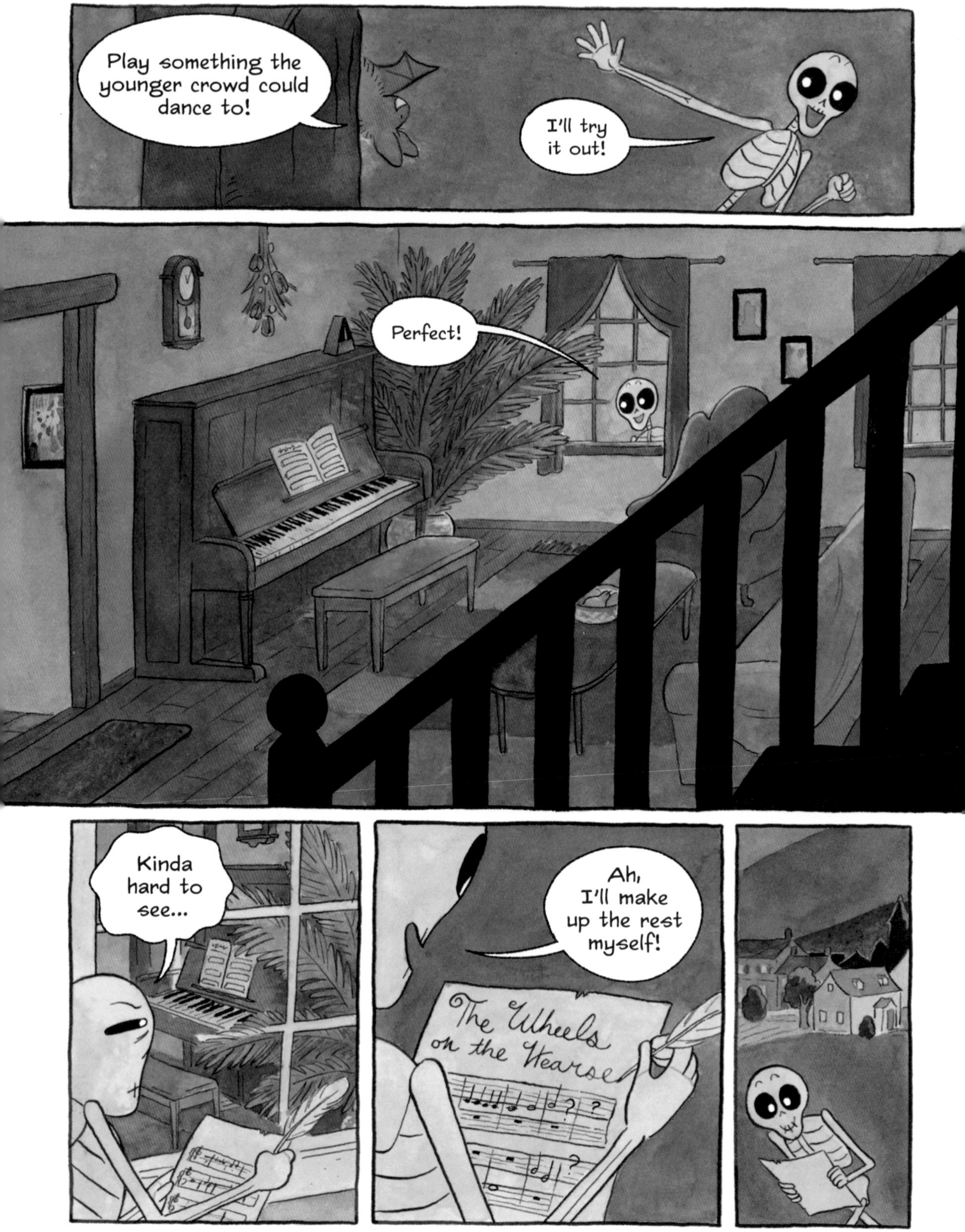
Play something the younger crowd could dance to!
I'll try it out!
Perfect!
Kinda hard to see...
Ah, I'll make up the rest myself!
The Wheels on the Hearse

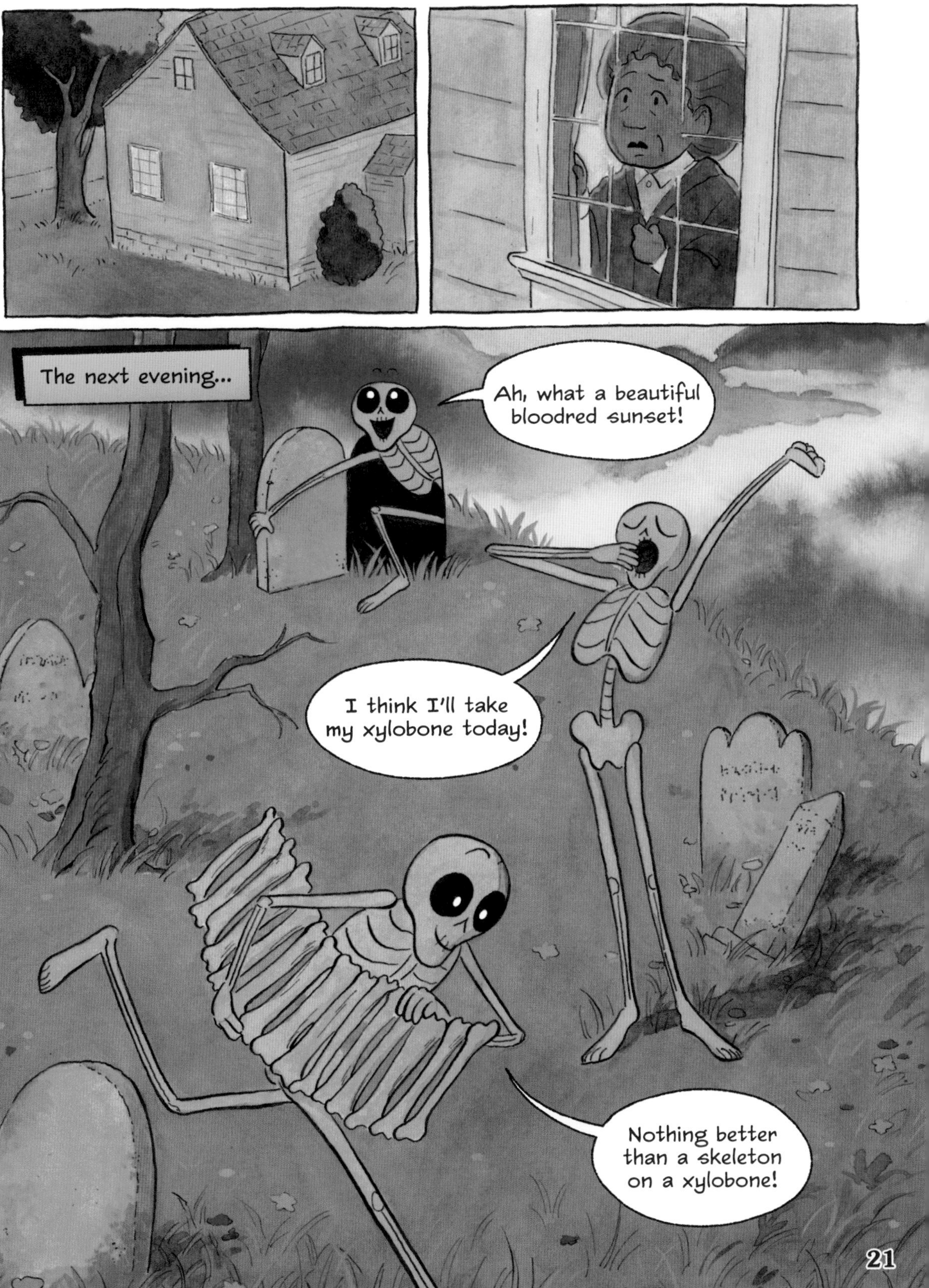

The next evening...
Ah, what a beautiful bloodred sunset!
I think I'll take my xylobone today!
Nothing better than a skeleton on a xylobone!

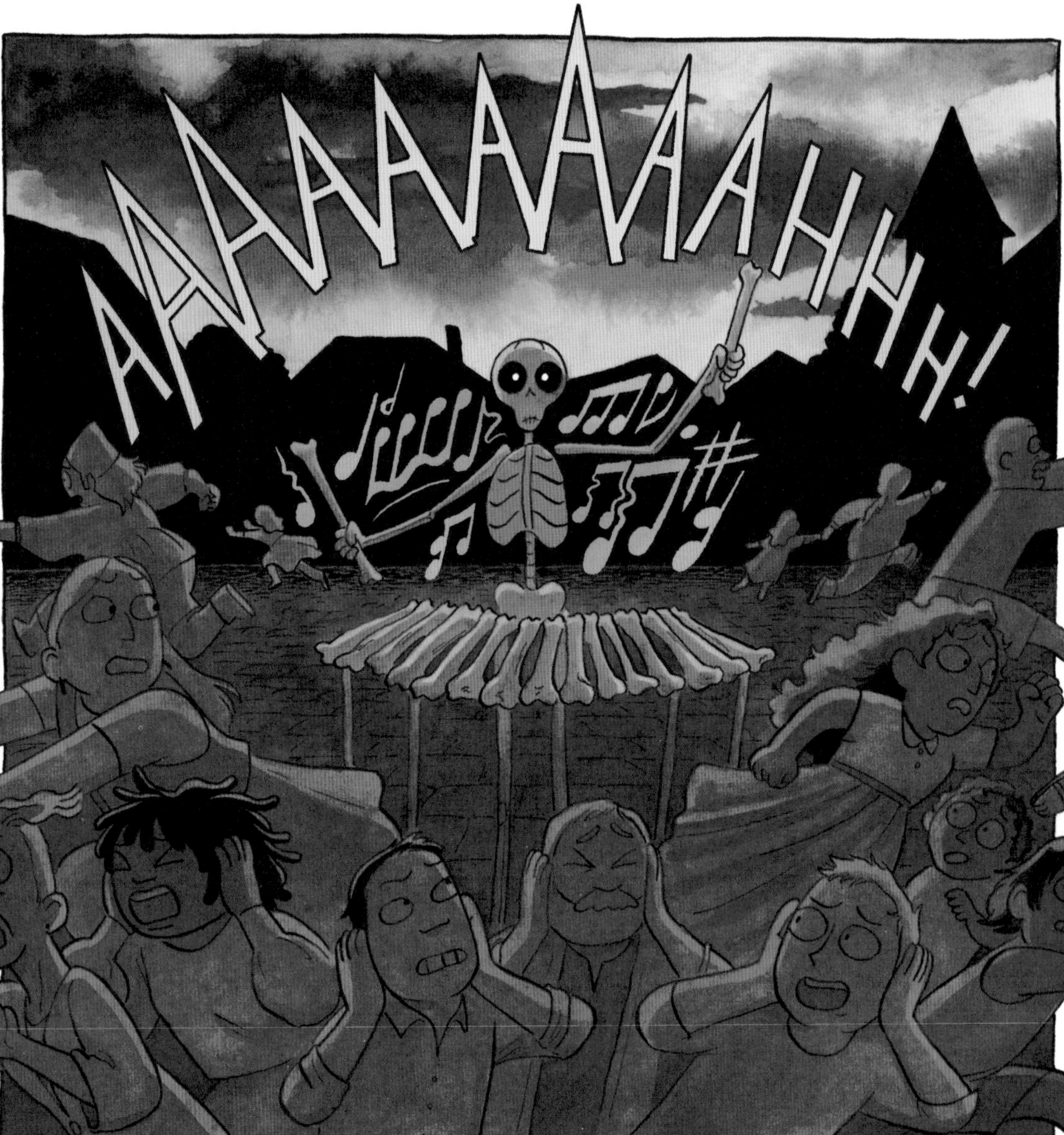
AAAAAAAAAHHHH!

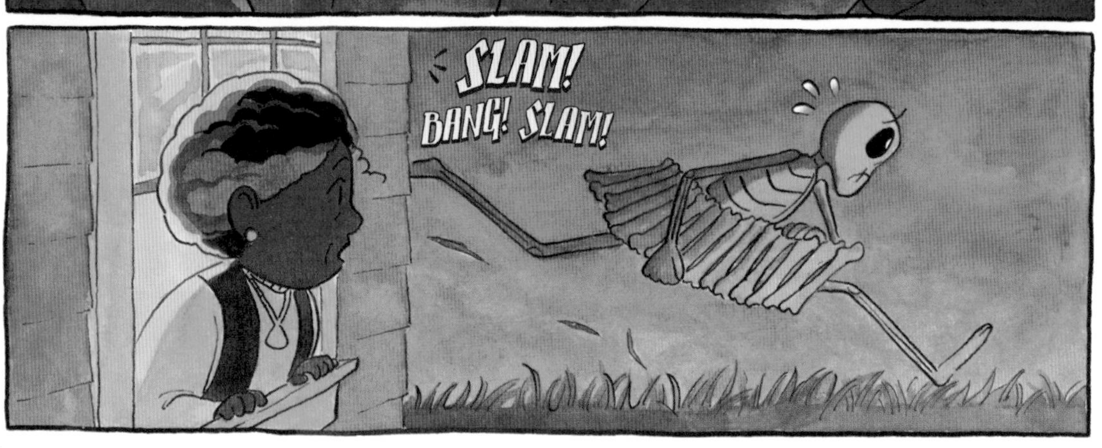
SLAM!
BANG! SLAM!

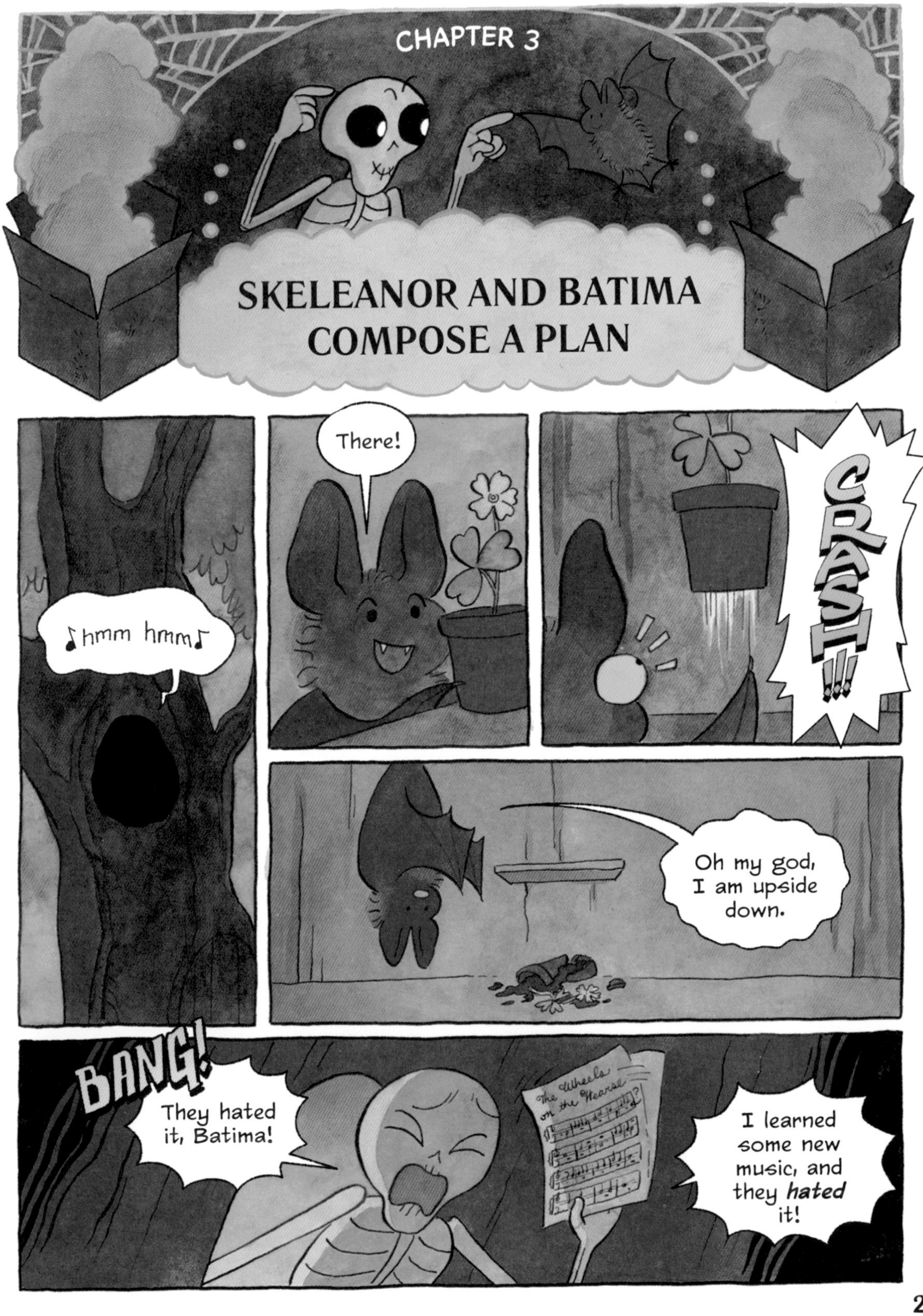
CHAPTER 3
SKELEANOR AND BATIMA COMPOSE A PLAN
♪hmm hmm♪
There!
CRASH!!!
Oh my god, I am upside down.
BANG!
They hated it, Batima!
The Wheels on the Hearse
I learned some new music, and they *hated* it!

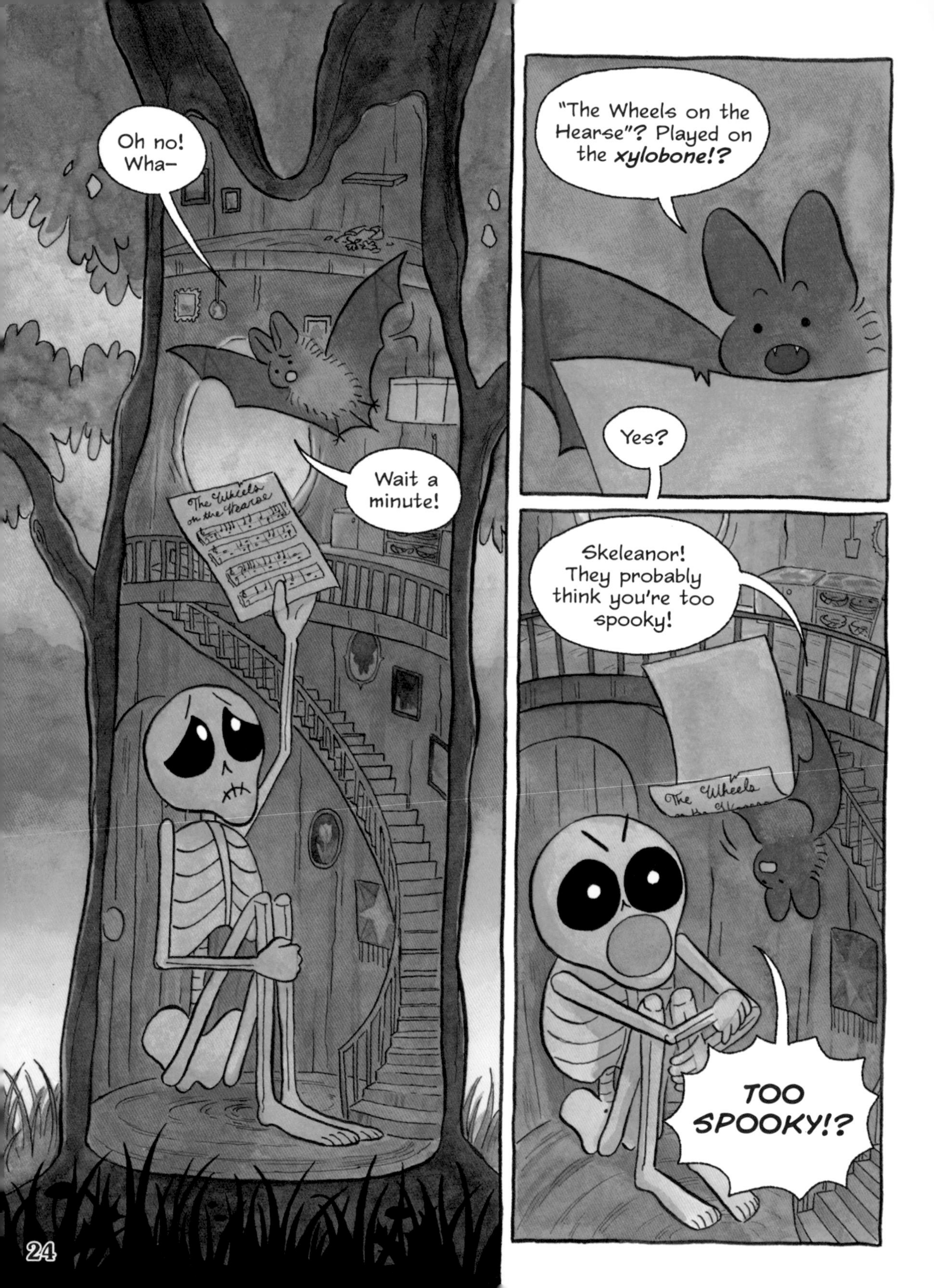
Oh no! Wha–
The Wheels on the Hearse
Wait a minute!
"The Wheels on the Hearse"? Played on the *xylobone!?*
Yes?
Skeleanor! They probably think you're too spooky!
The Wheels
TOO SPOOKY!?

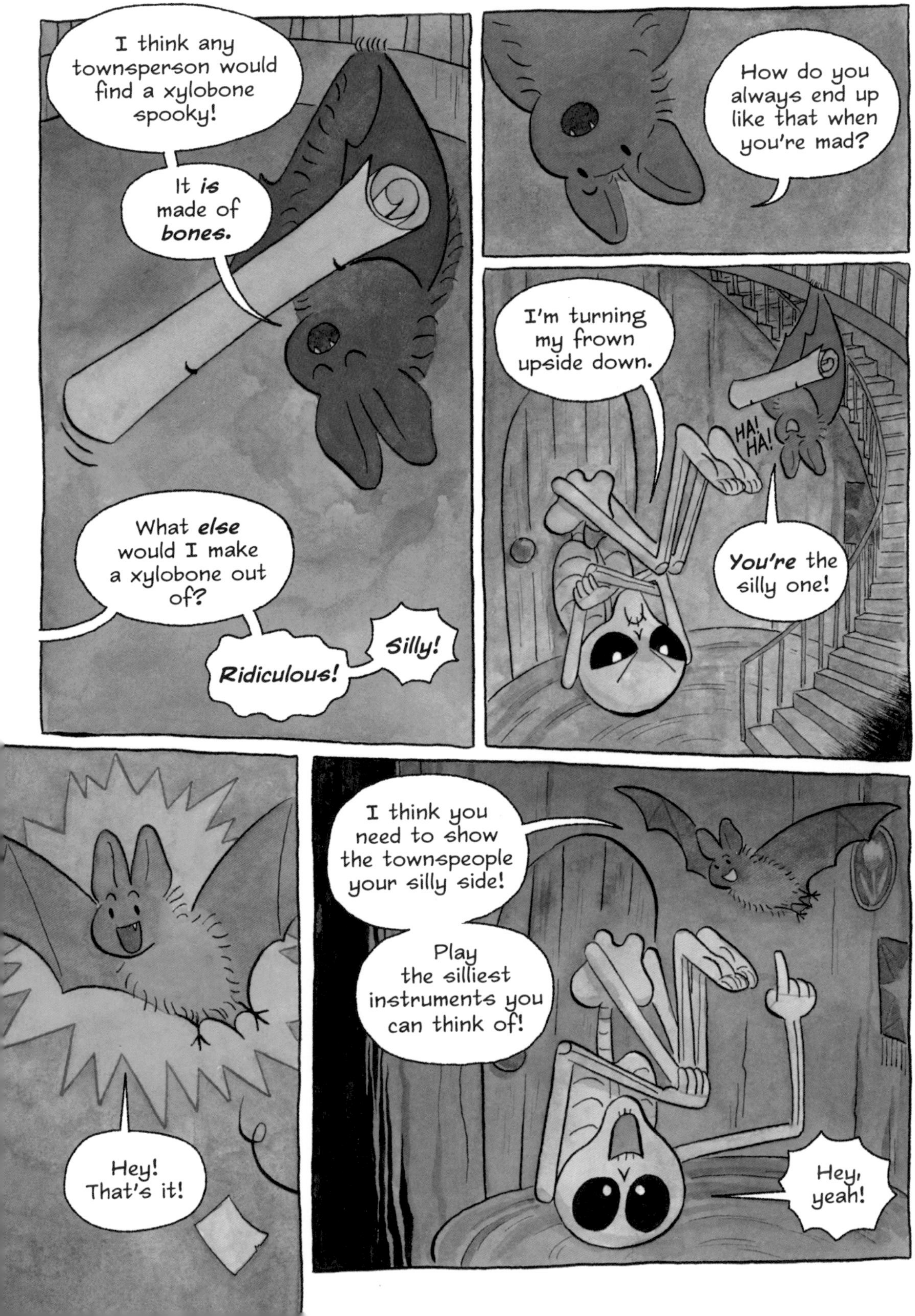

I think any townsperson would find a xylobone spooky!
It *is* made of **bones.**
What *else* would I make a xylobone out of?
Ridiculous!
Silly!
How do you always end up like that when you're mad?
I'm turning my frown upside down.
HA! HA!
You're the silly one!
Hey! That's it!
I think you need to show the townspeople your silly side!
Play the silliest instruments you can think of!
Hey, yeah!

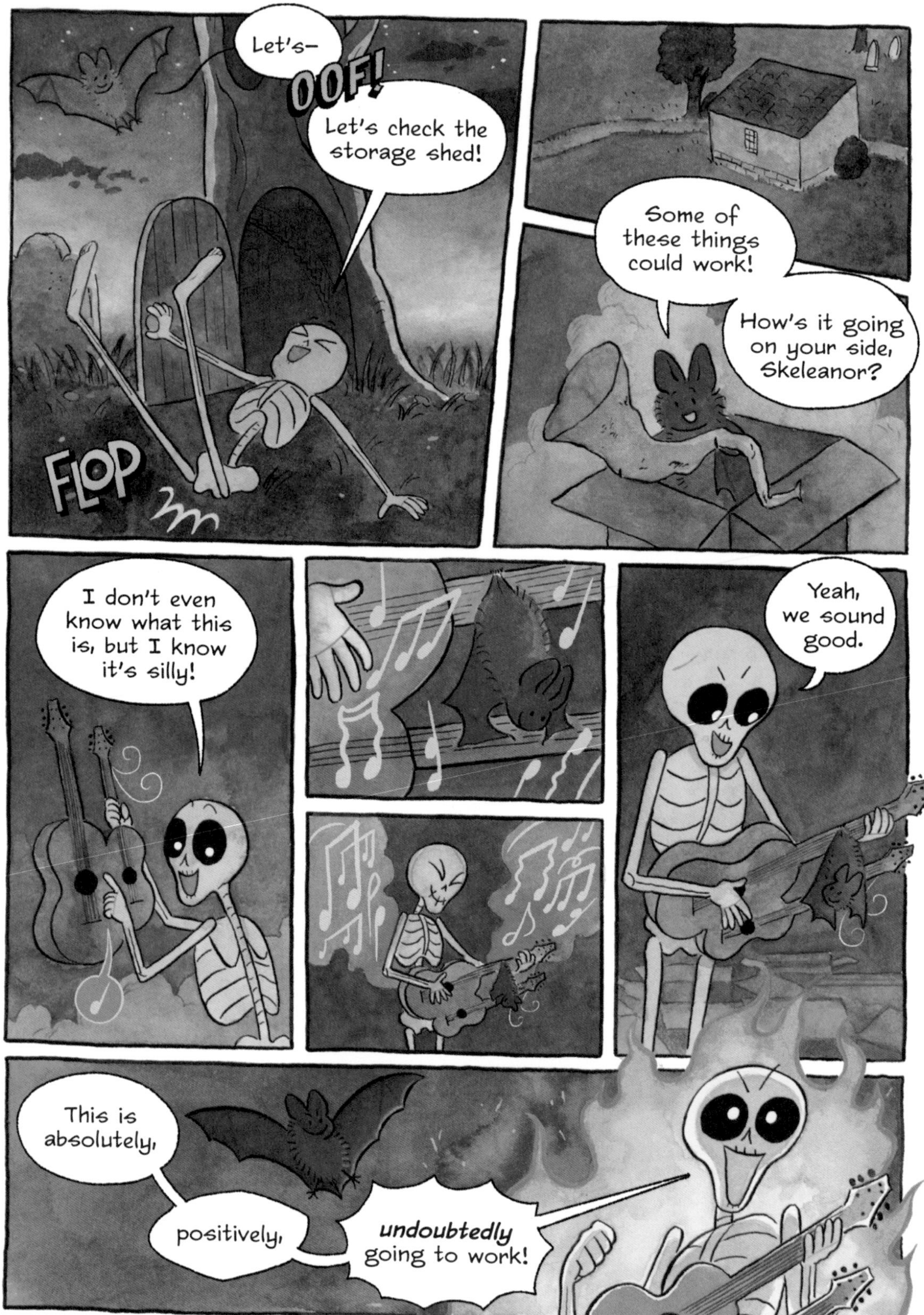
Let's—
OOF!
Let's check the storage shed!
FLOP
Some of these things could work!
How's it going on your side, Skeleanor?
I don't even know what this is, but I know it's silly!
Yeah, we sound good.
This is absolutely,
positively,
undoubtedly going to work!

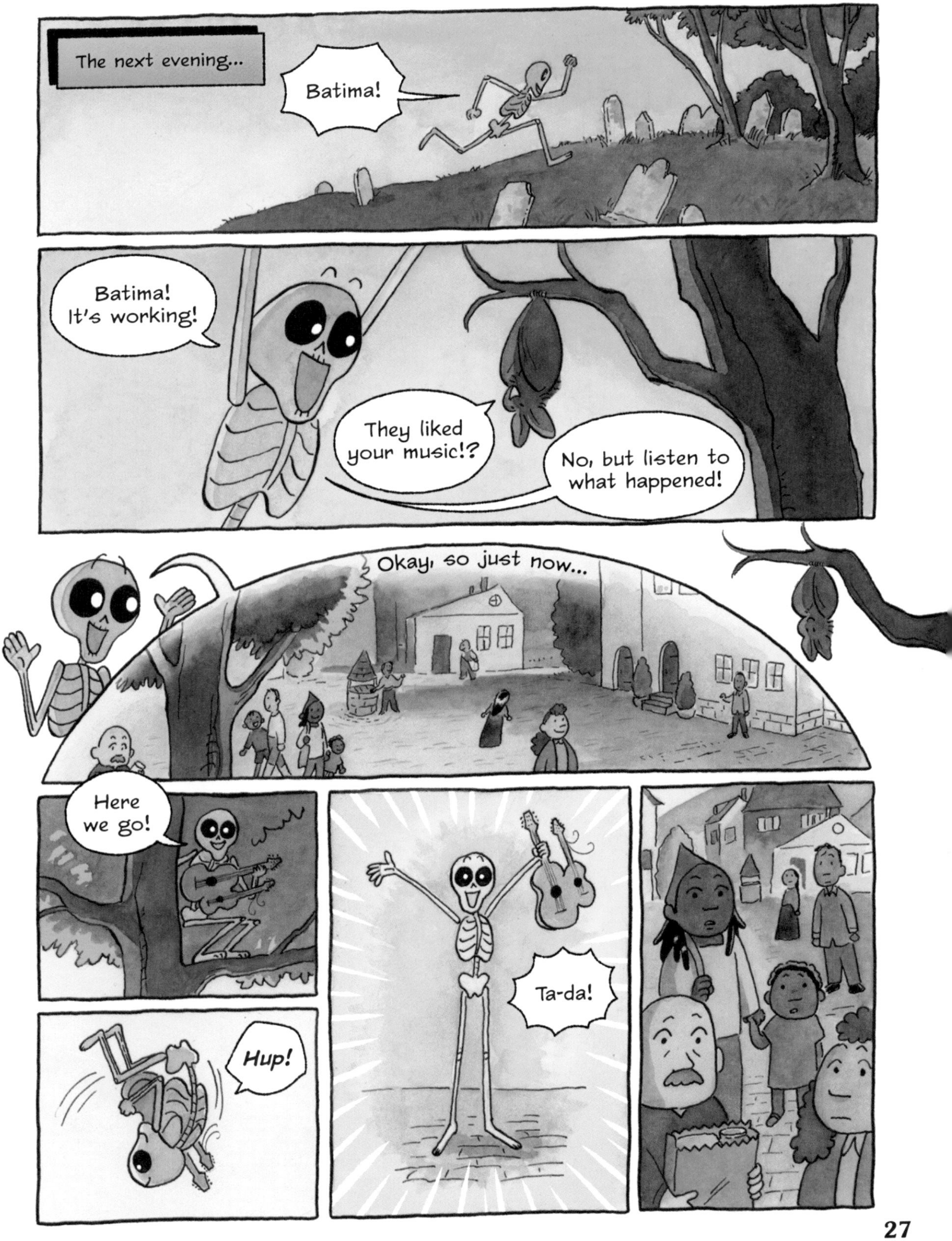
The next evening...
Batima!
Batima! It's working!
They liked your music!?
No, but listen to what happened!
Okay, so just now...
Here we go!
Hup!
Ta-da!

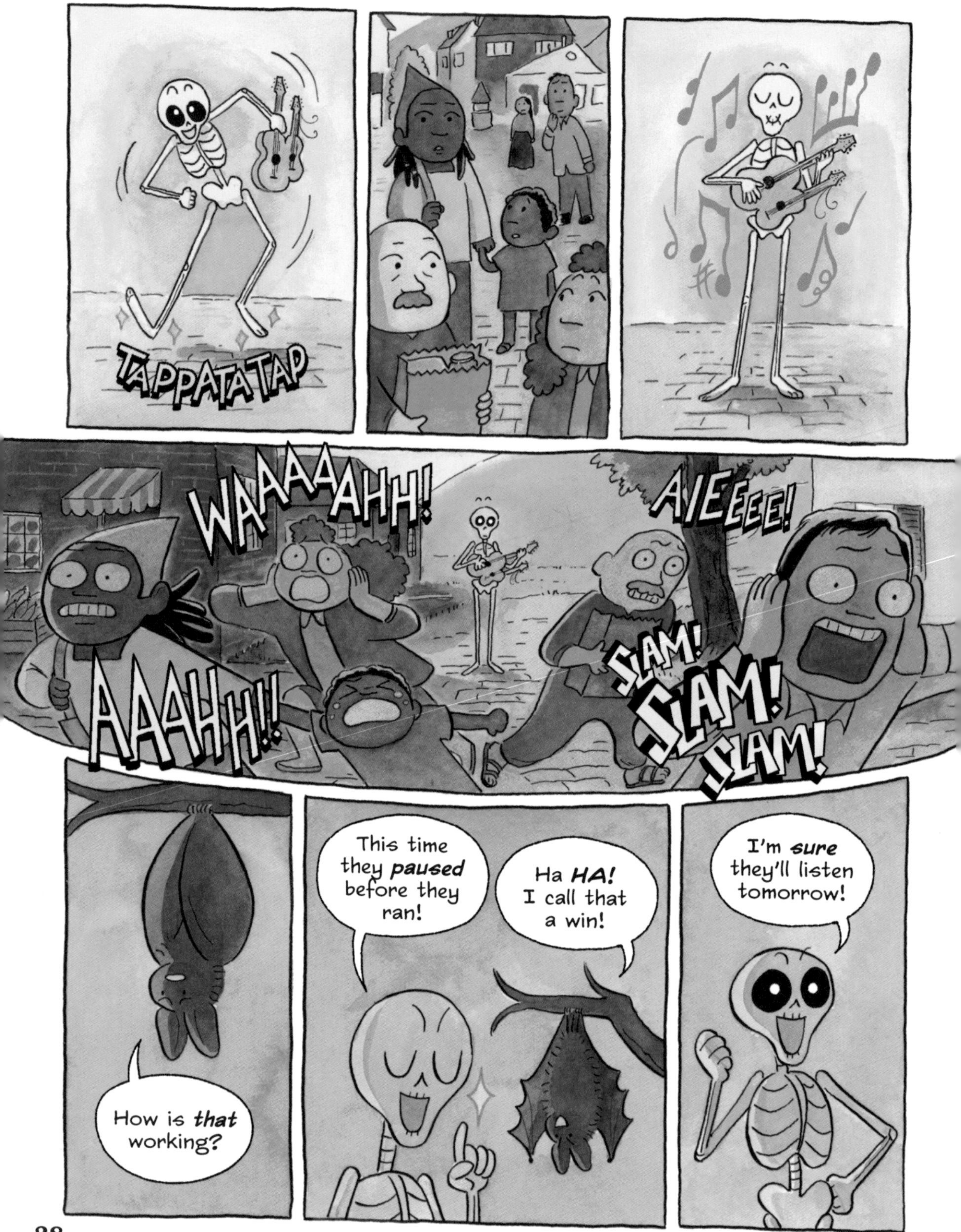
TAPPATATAP
WAAAAAAHH!
AIEEEEE!
AAAHH!!
SLAM!
SLAM!
SLAM!
How is *that* working?
This time they ***paused*** before they ran!
Ha ***HA!*** I call that a win!
I'm ***sure*** they'll listen tomorrow!

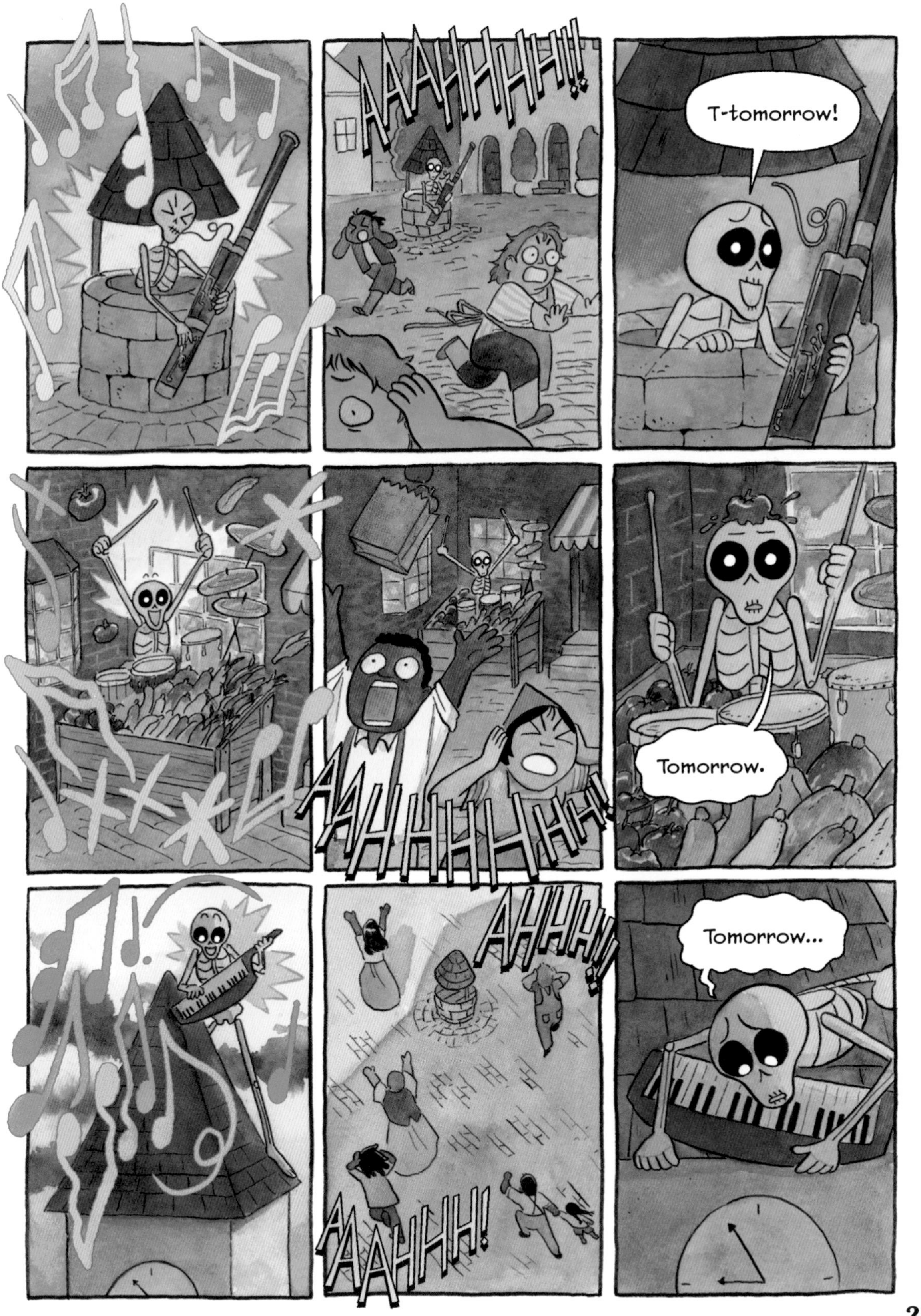
AAAHHHHH!!
T-tomorrow!
AAHHHHHHH!
Tomorrow.
AHHHH!
AAHHH!
Tomorrow...

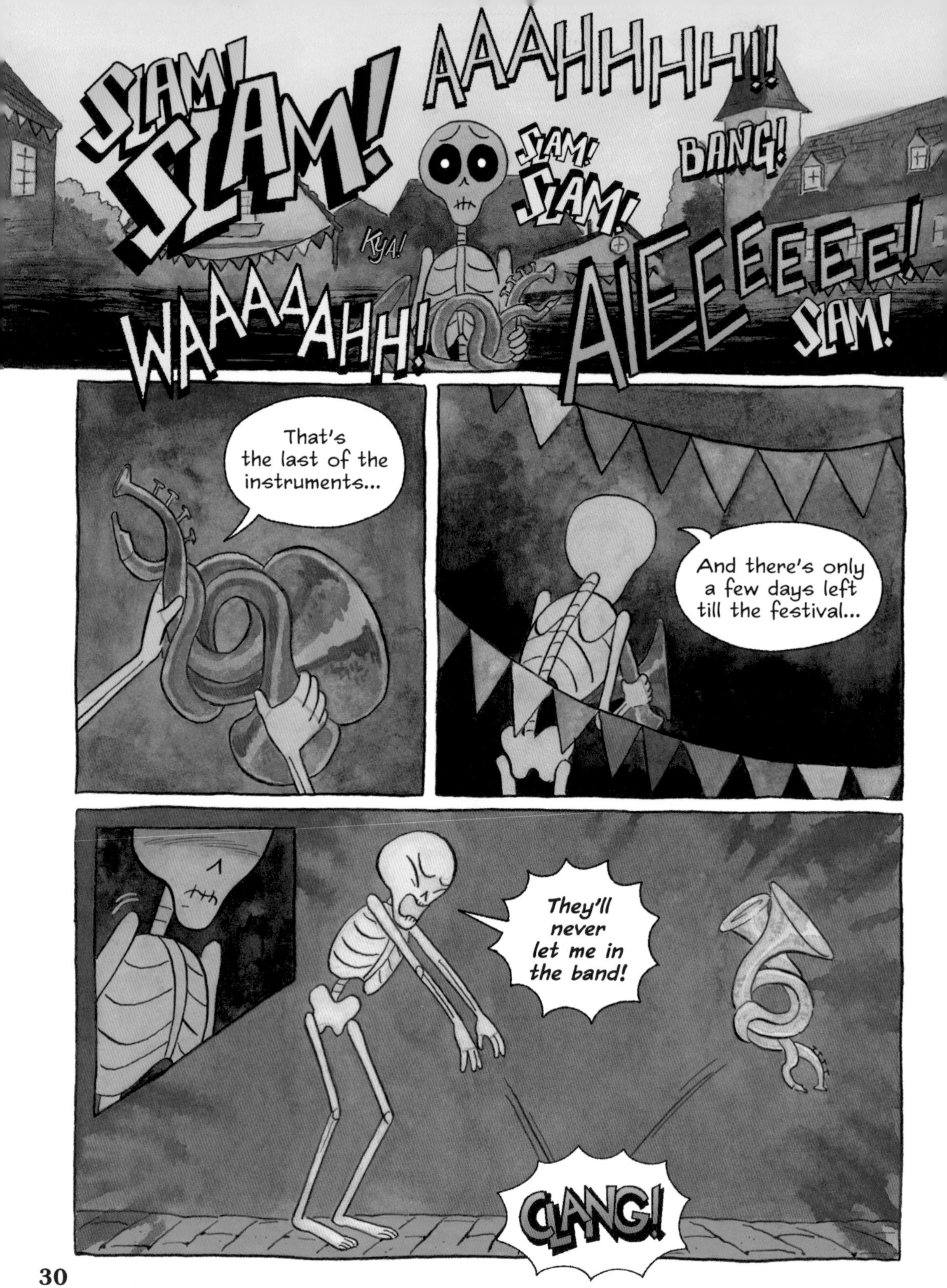
SLAM!
SLAM!
AAAHHHH!!
SLAM!
SLAM!
BANG!
KYA!
WAAAAAHH!
AIEEEEEEE!
SLAM!
That's the last of the instruments...
And there's only a few days left till the festival...
They'll never let me in the band!
CLANG!

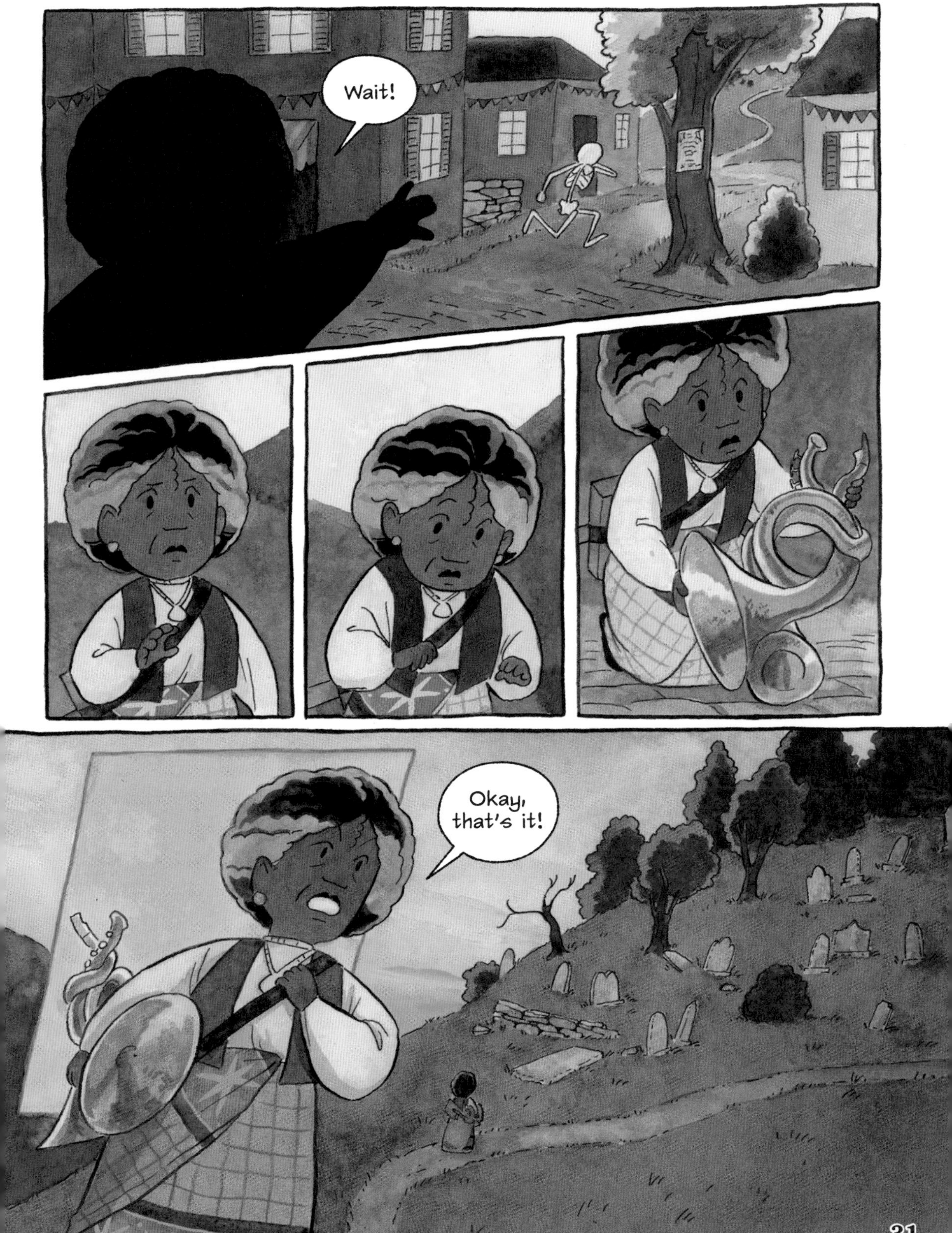
Wait!
Okay, that's it!

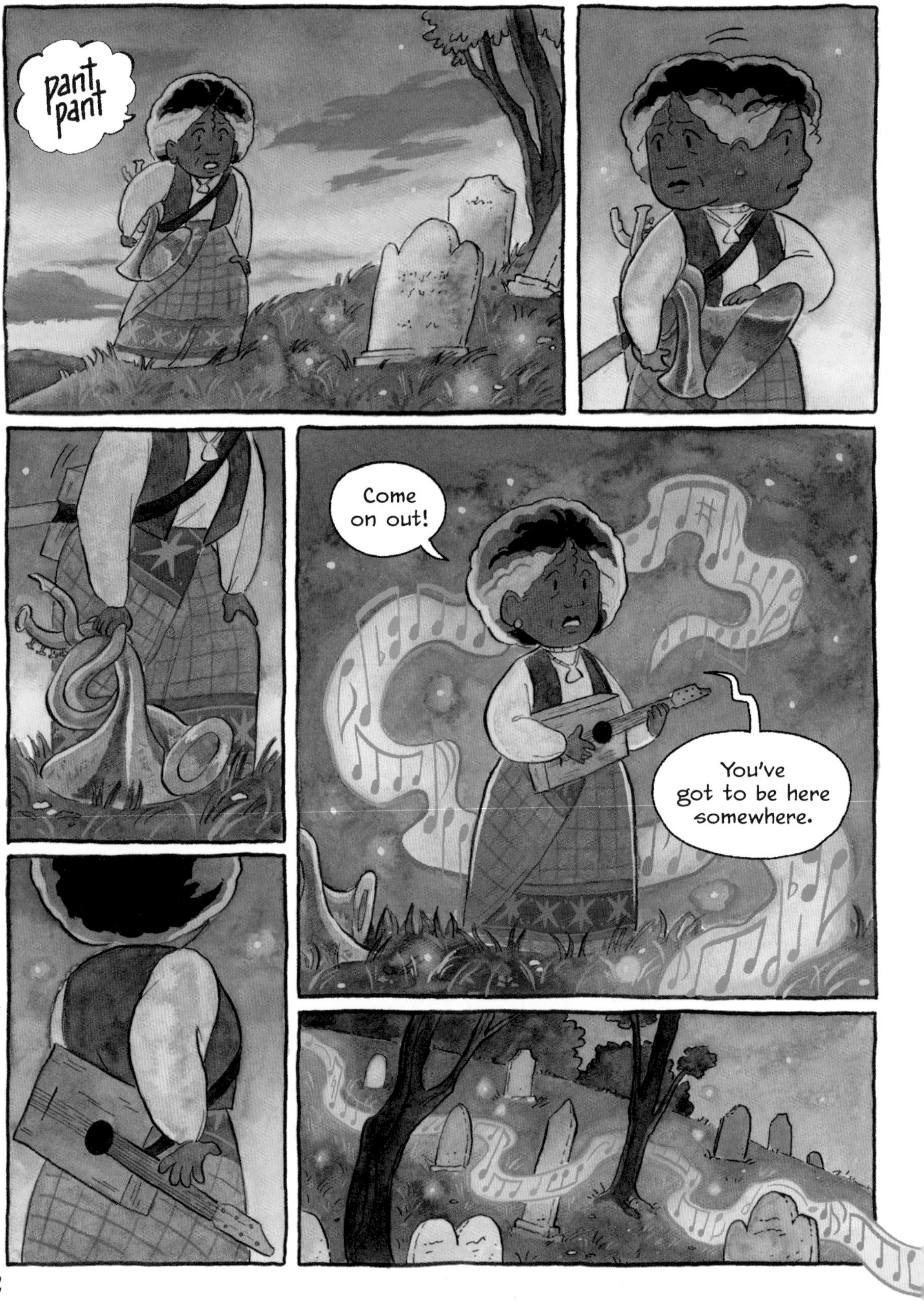
pant pant
Come on out!
You've got to be here somewhere.

SOB

SOB

SOB

SOB

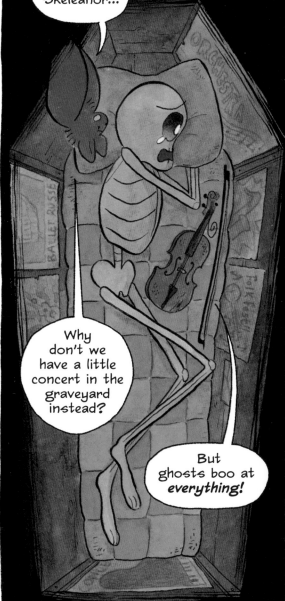

I'm sorry, Skeleanor...

Why don't we have a little concert in the graveyard instead?

But ghosts boo at *everything!*

I wanted to play in the band because I thought it'd be fun...

...but now I don't want to play at all...

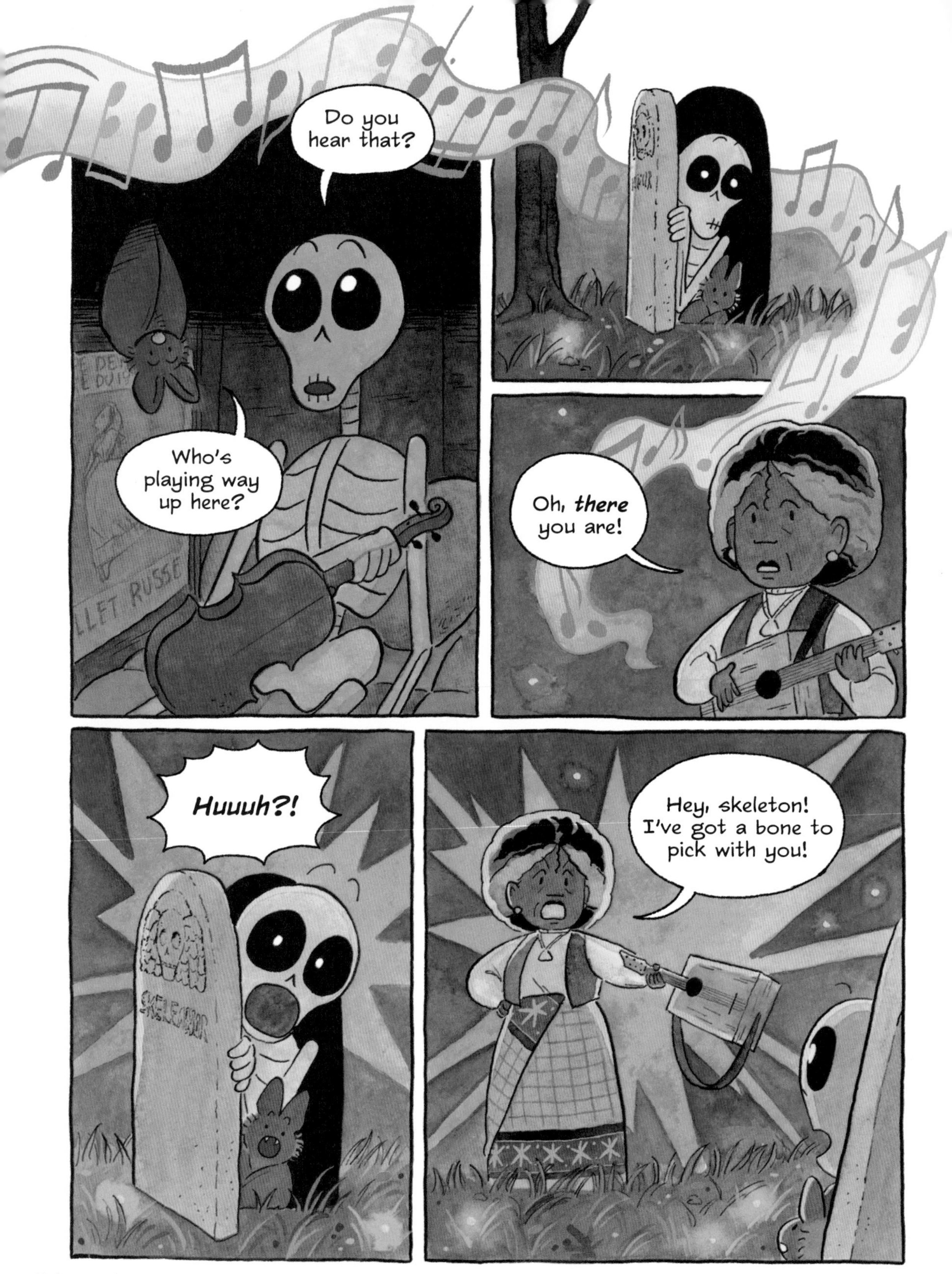
Do you hear that?
Who's playing way up here?
Oh, *there* you are!
Huuuh?!
Hey, skeleton! I've got a bone to pick with you!

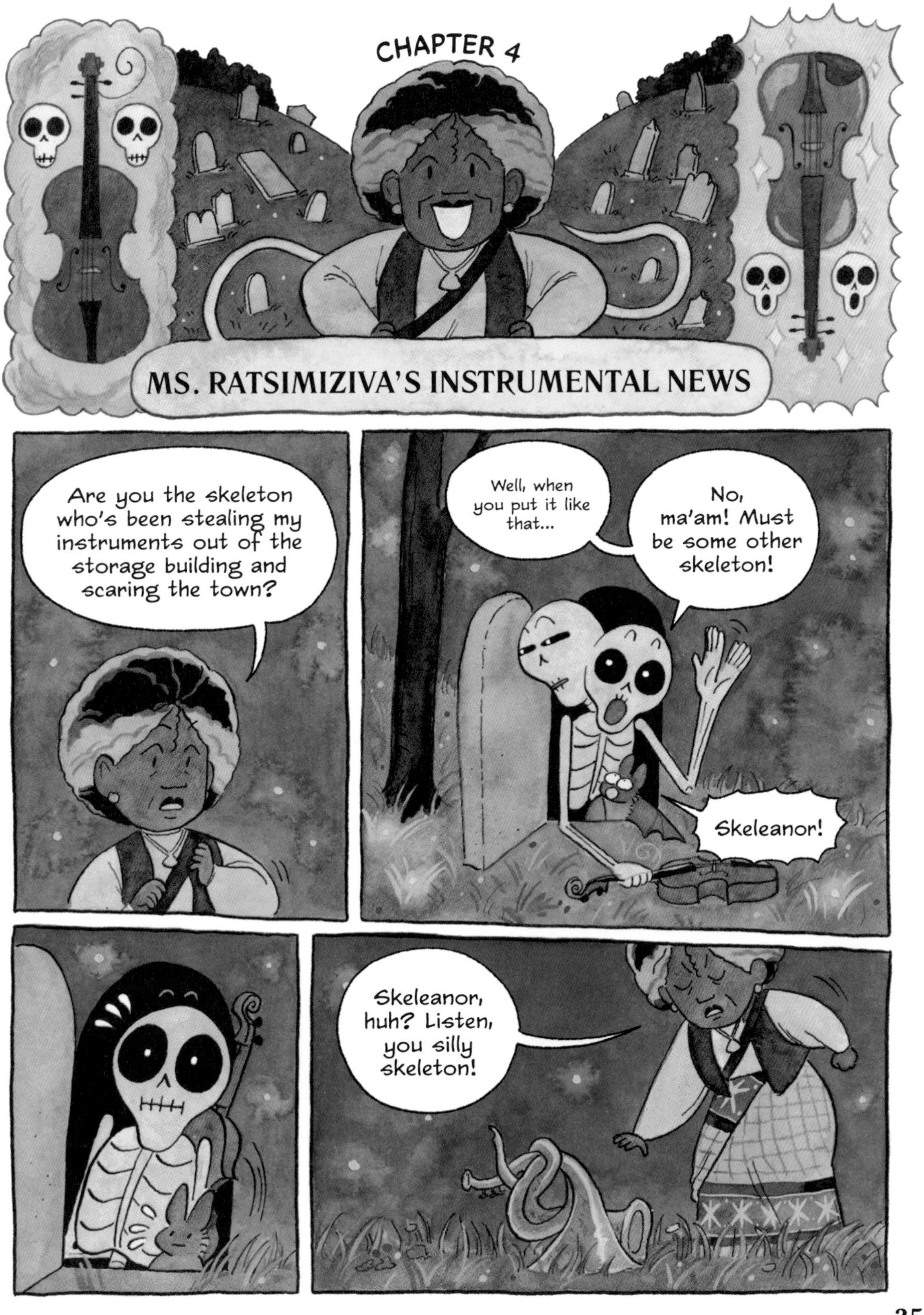
CHAPTER 4
MS. RATSIMIZIVA'S INSTRUMENTAL NEWS
Are you the skeleton who's been stealing my instruments out of the storage building and scaring the town?
No, ma'am! Must be some other skeleton!
Well, when you put it like that...
Skeleanor!
Skeleanor, huh? Listen, you silly skeleton!

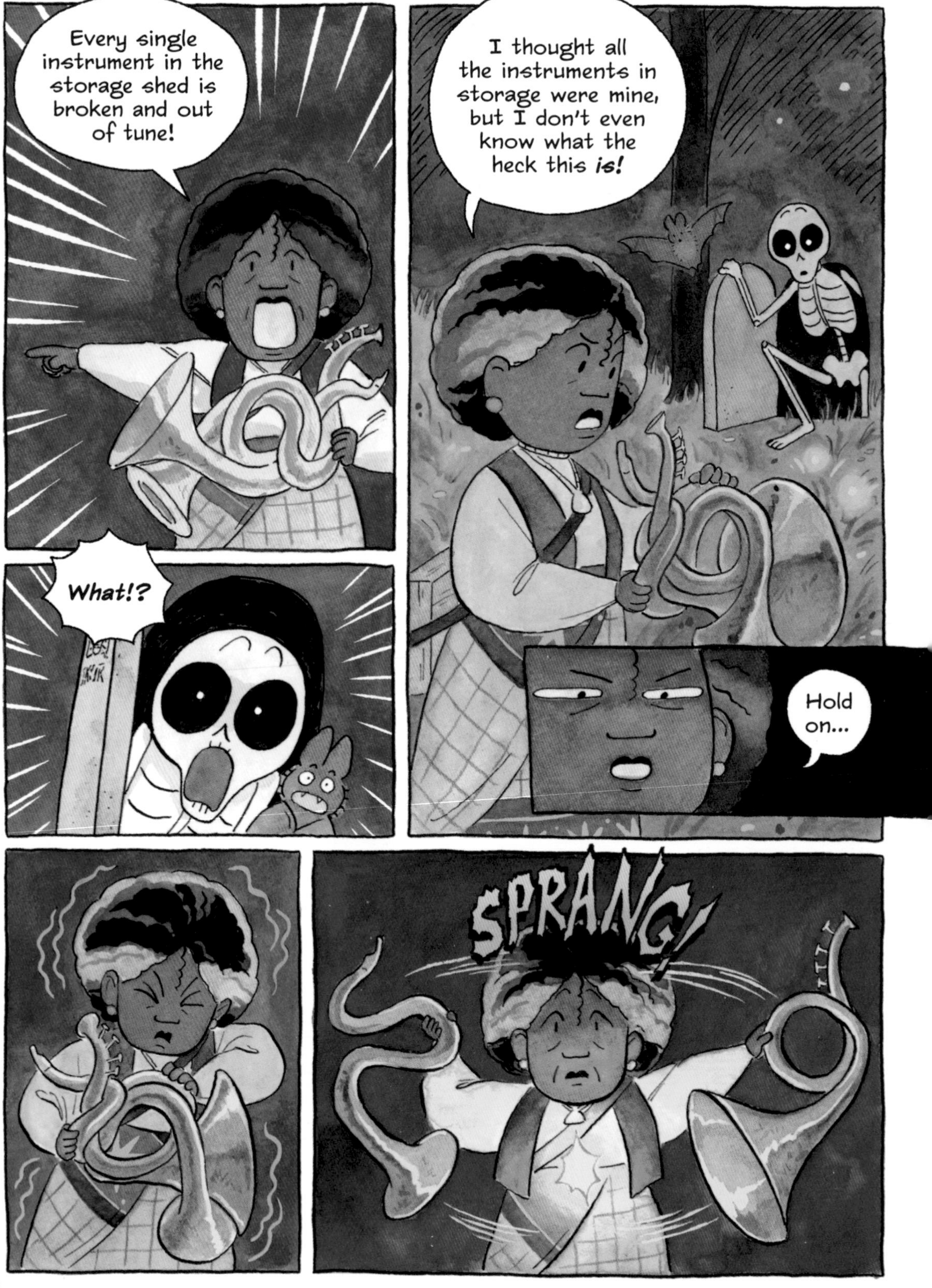

Every single instrument in the storage shed is broken and out of tune!
What!?
I thought all the instruments in storage were mine, but I don't even know what the heck this *is!*
Hold on...
SPRANG!

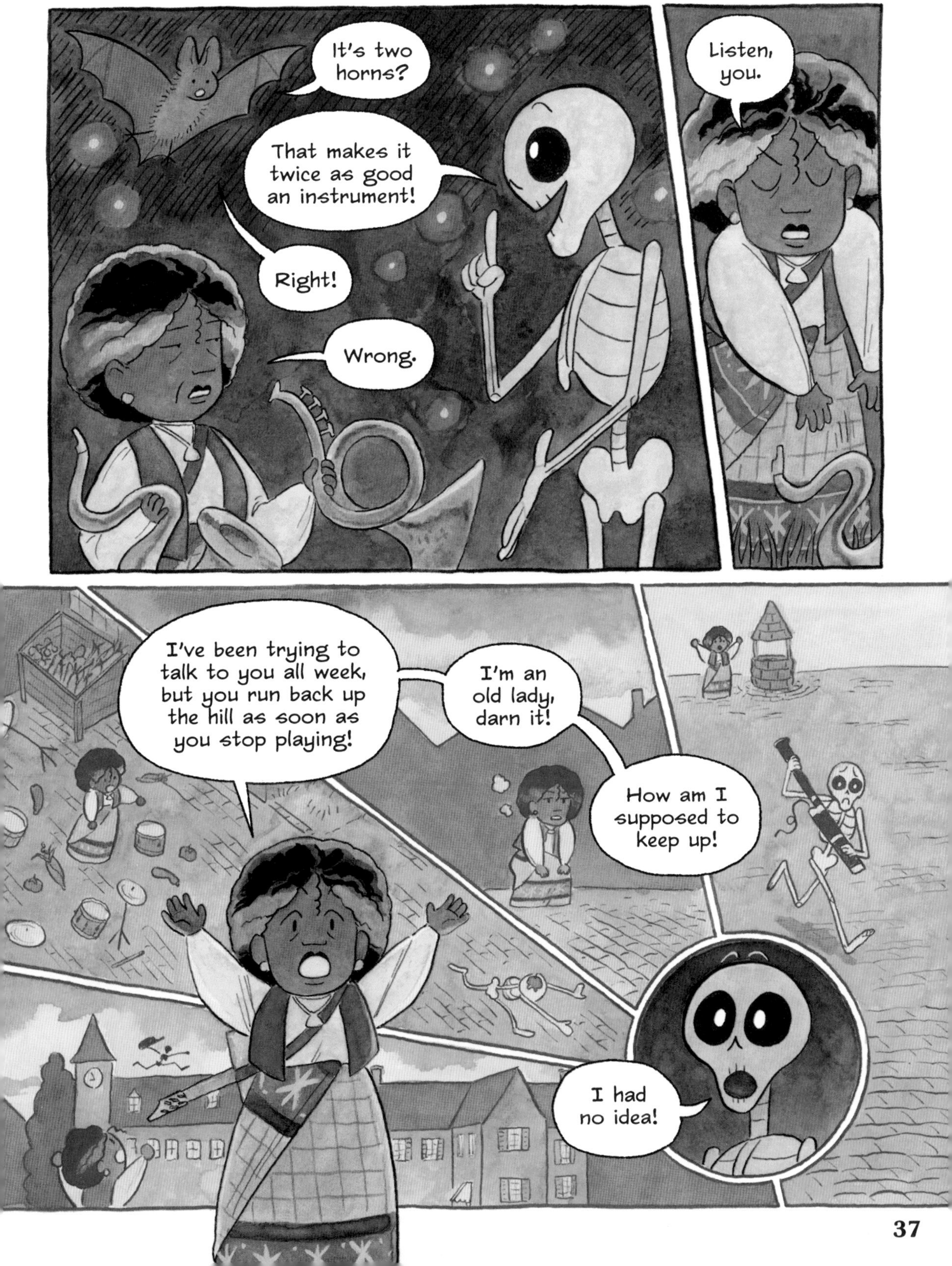
It's two horns?
That makes it twice as good an instrument!
Right!
Wrong.
Listen, you.
I've been trying to talk to you all week, but you run back up the hill as soon as you stop playing!
I'm an old lady, darn it!
How am I supposed to keep up!
I had no idea!

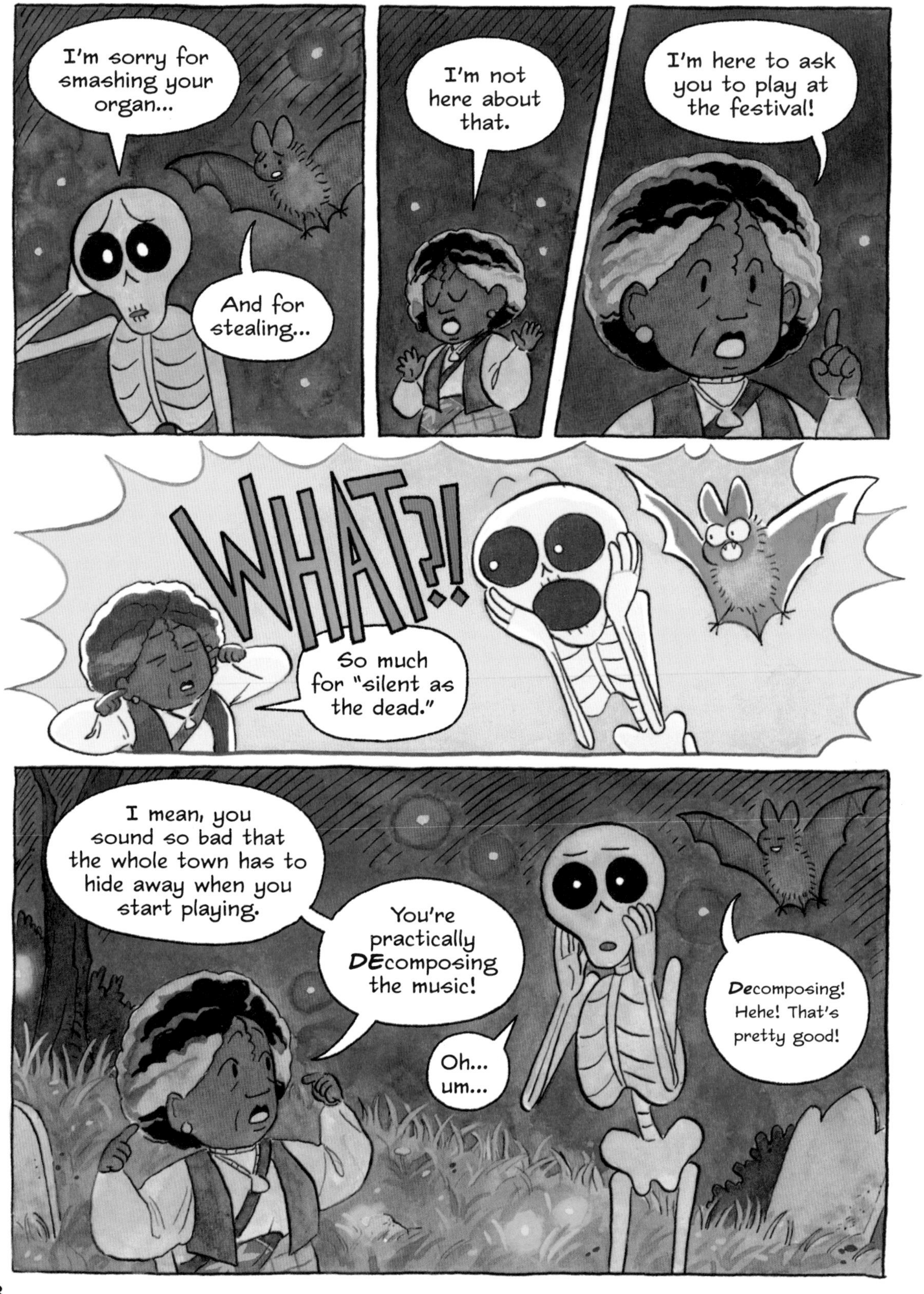
I'm sorry for smashing your organ...
And for stealing...
I'm not here about that.
I'm here to ask you to play at the festival!
WHAT?!
So much for "silent as the dead."
I mean, you sound so bad that the whole town has to hide away when you start playing.
You're practically DEcomposing the music!
Oh... um...
Decomposing! Hehe! That's pretty good!

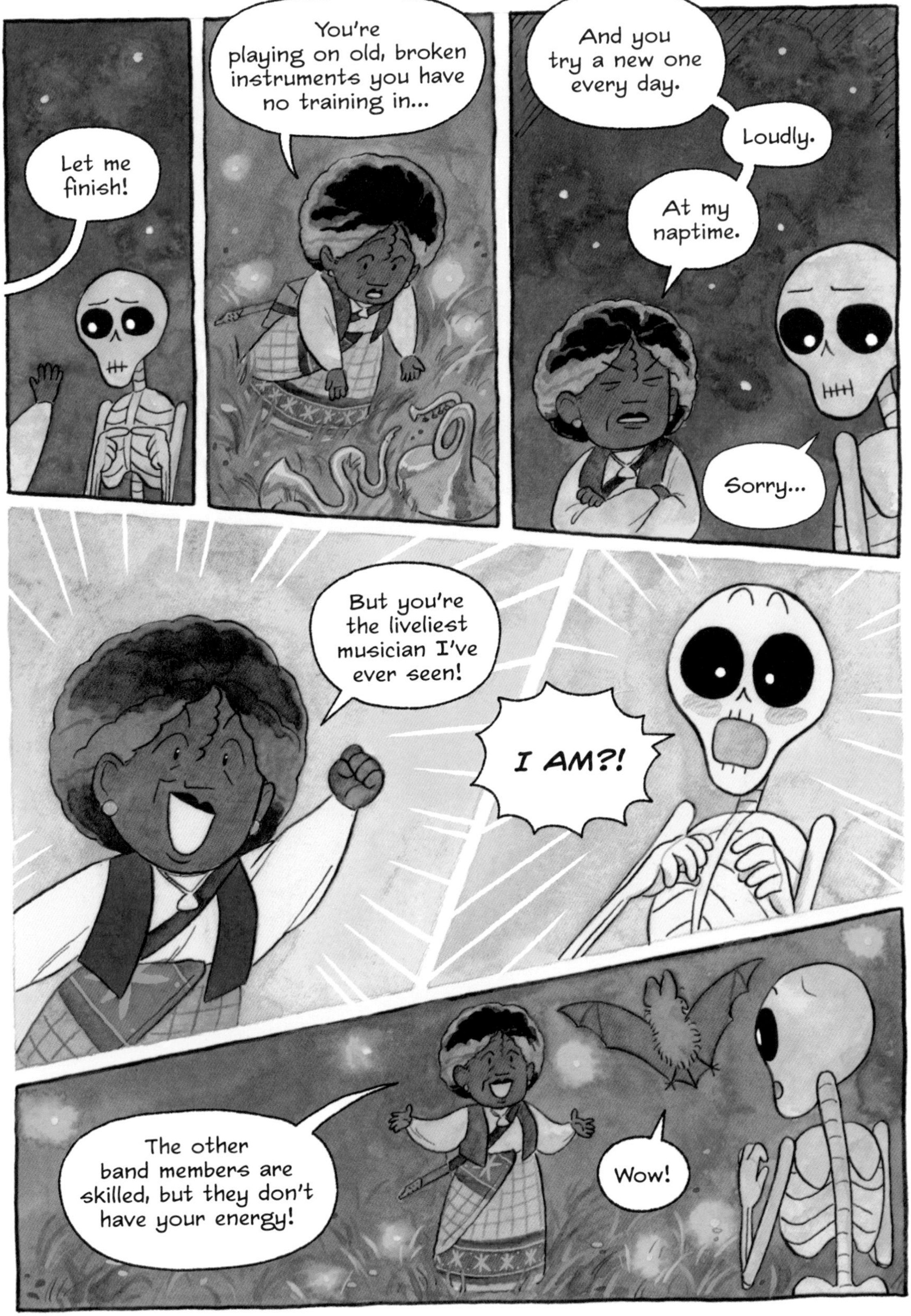
Let me finish!
You're playing on old, broken instruments you have no training in...
And you try a new one every day.
Loudly.
At my naptime.
Sorry...
But you're the liveliest musician I've ever seen!
I AM?!
The other band members are skilled, but they don't have your energy!
Wow!

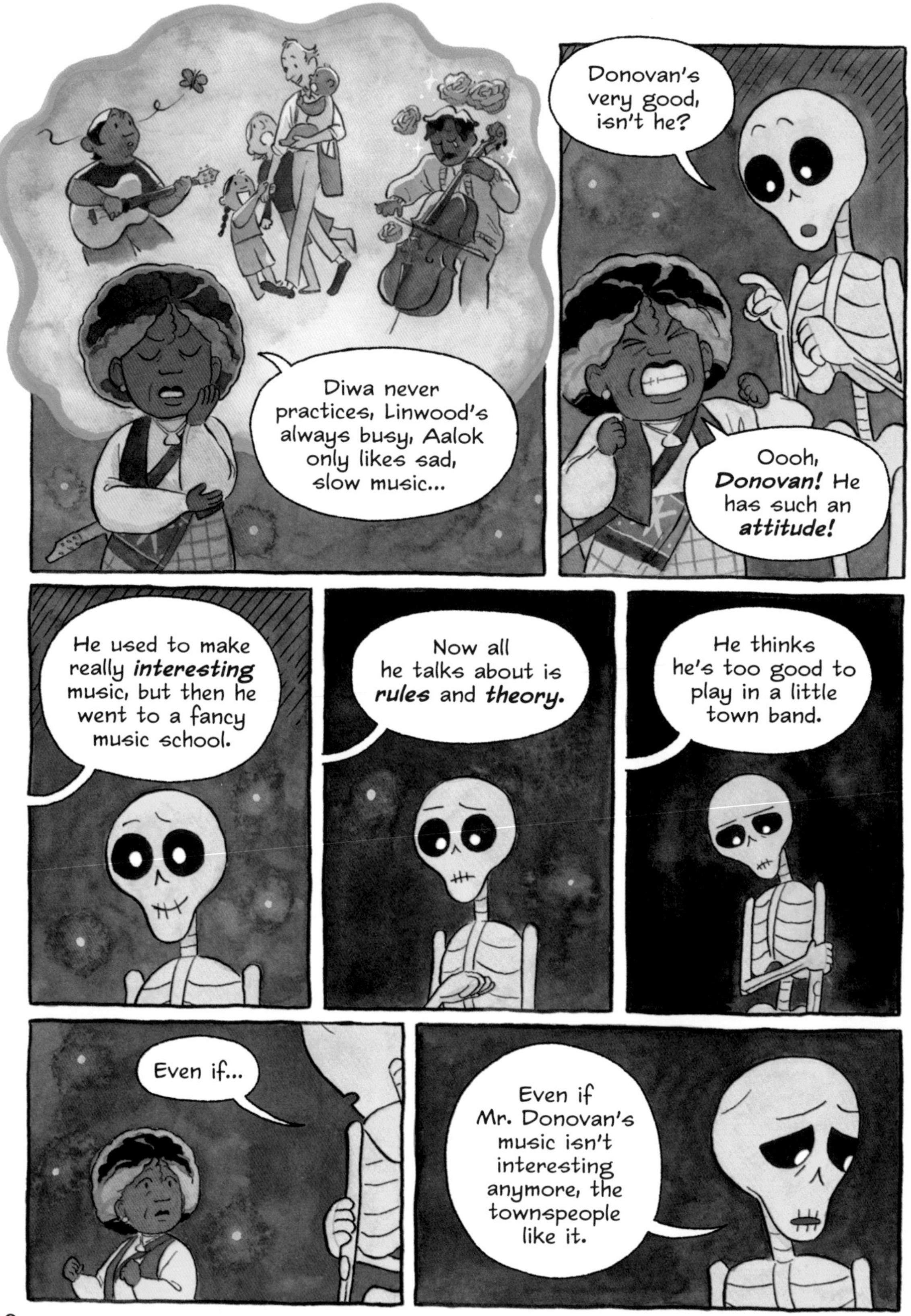
Diwa never practices, Linwood's always busy, Aalok only likes sad, slow music...
Donovan's very good, isn't he?
Oooh, **Donovan!** He has such an ***attitude!***
He used to make really ***interesting*** music, but then he went to a fancy music school.
Now all he talks about is ***rules*** and ***theory.***
He thinks he's too good to play in a little town band.
Even if...
Even if Mr. Donovan's music isn't interesting anymore, the townspeople like it.

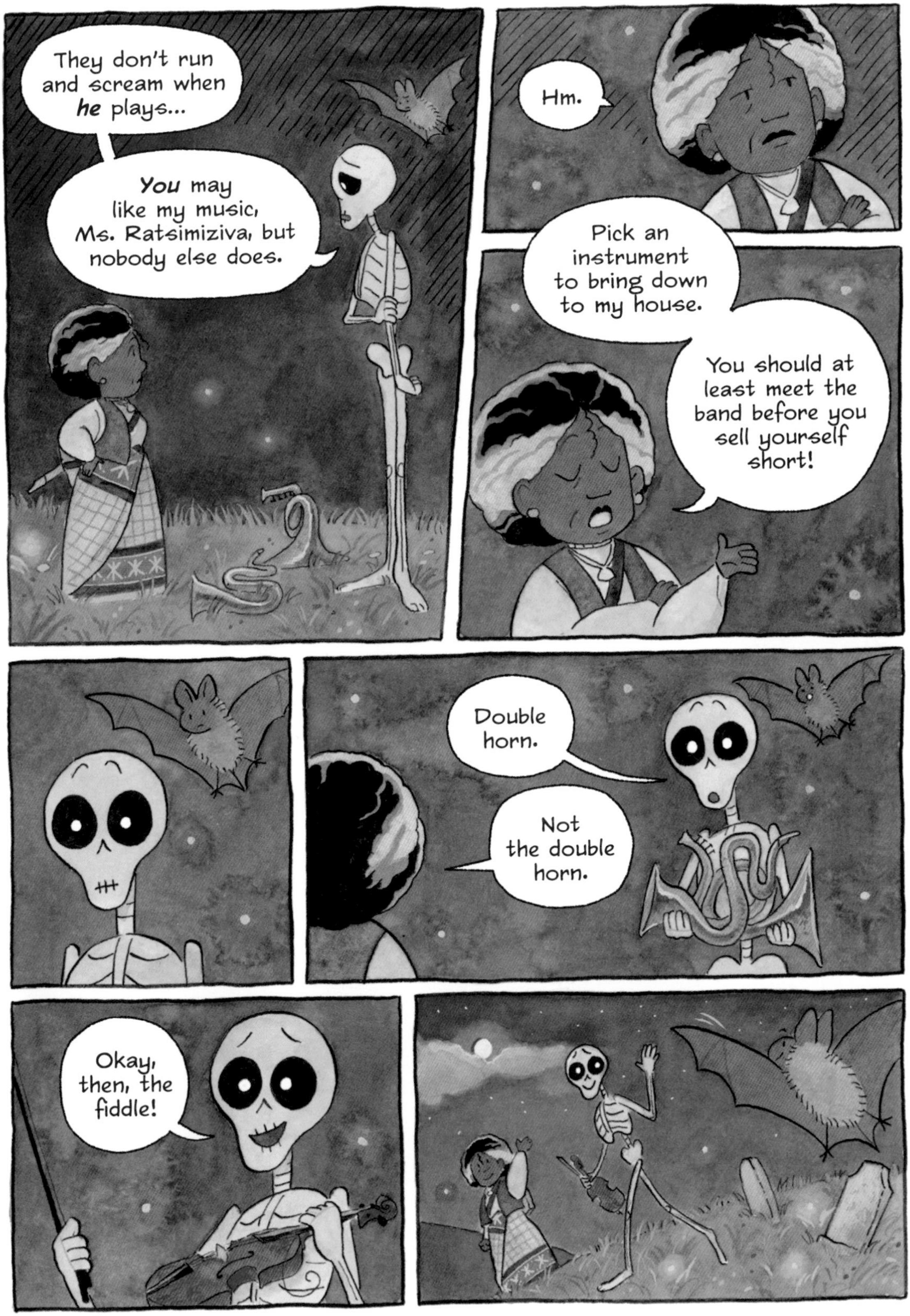
They don't run and scream when *he* plays...
You may like my music, Ms. Ratsimiziva, but nobody else does.
Hm.
Pick an instrument to bring down to my house.
You should at least meet the band before you sell yourself short!
Double horn.
Not the double horn.
Okay, then, the fiddle!

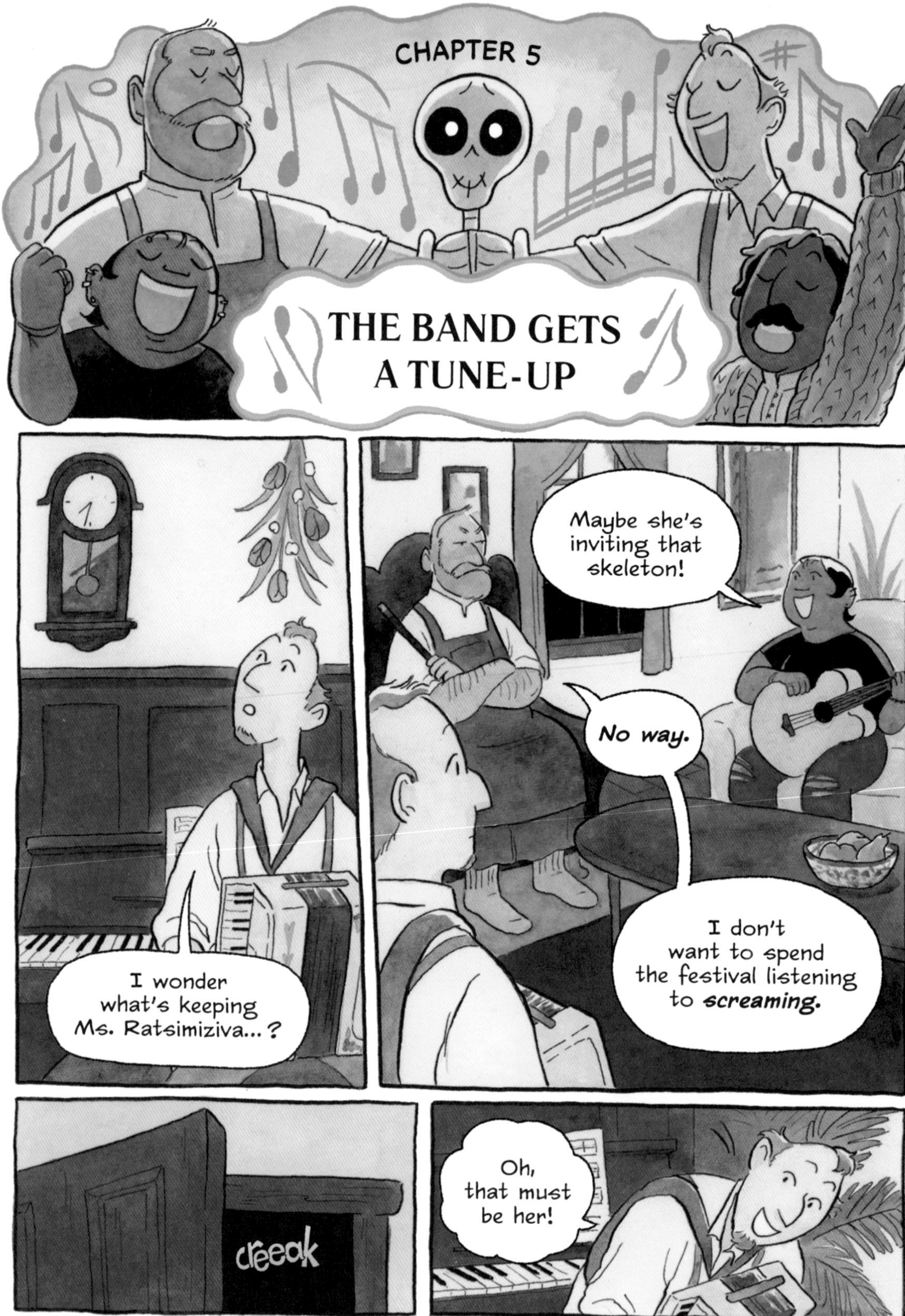
CHAPTER 5
THE BAND GETS A TUNE-UP
I wonder what's keeping Ms. Ratsimiziva...?
Maybe she's inviting that skeleton!
No way.
I don't want to spend the festival listening to screaming.
creeak
Oh, that must be her!

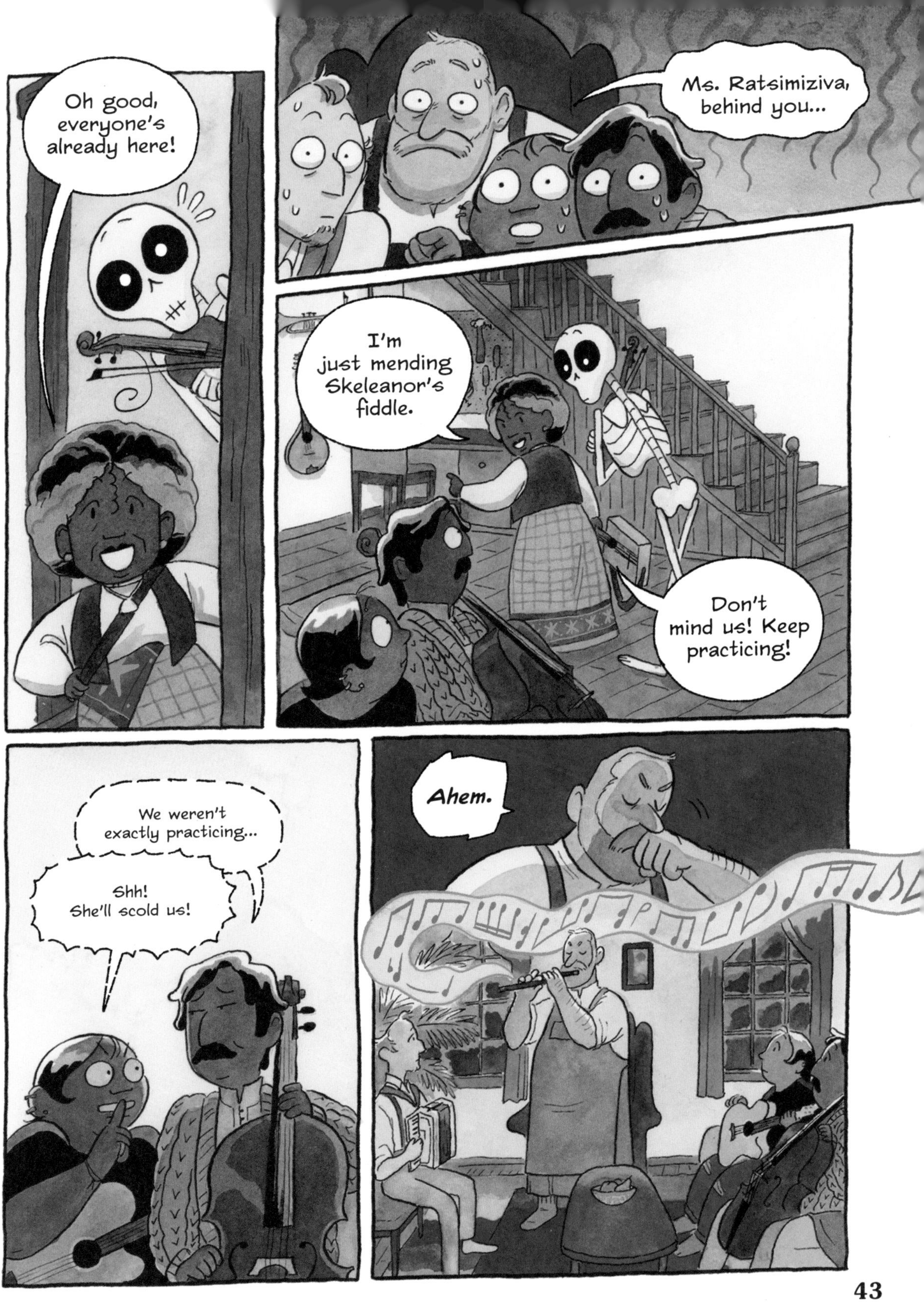
Oh good, everyone's already here!
Ms. Ratsimiziva, behind you...
I'm just mending Skeleanor's fiddle.
Don't mind us! Keep practicing!
We weren't exactly practicing...
Shh! She'll scold us!
Ahem.

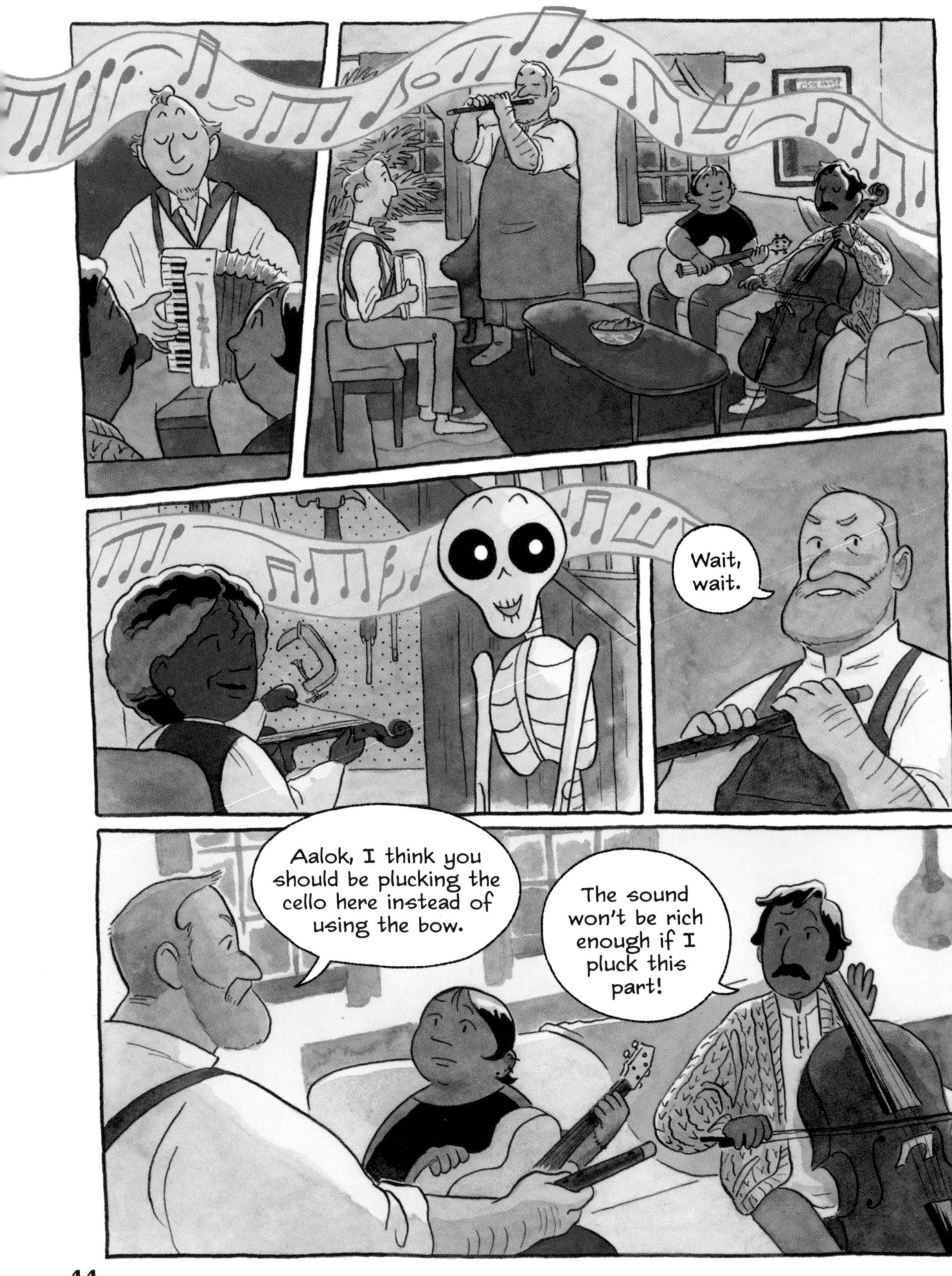
Wait, wait.
Aalok, I think you should be plucking the cello here instead of using the bow.
The sound won't be rich enough if I pluck this part!

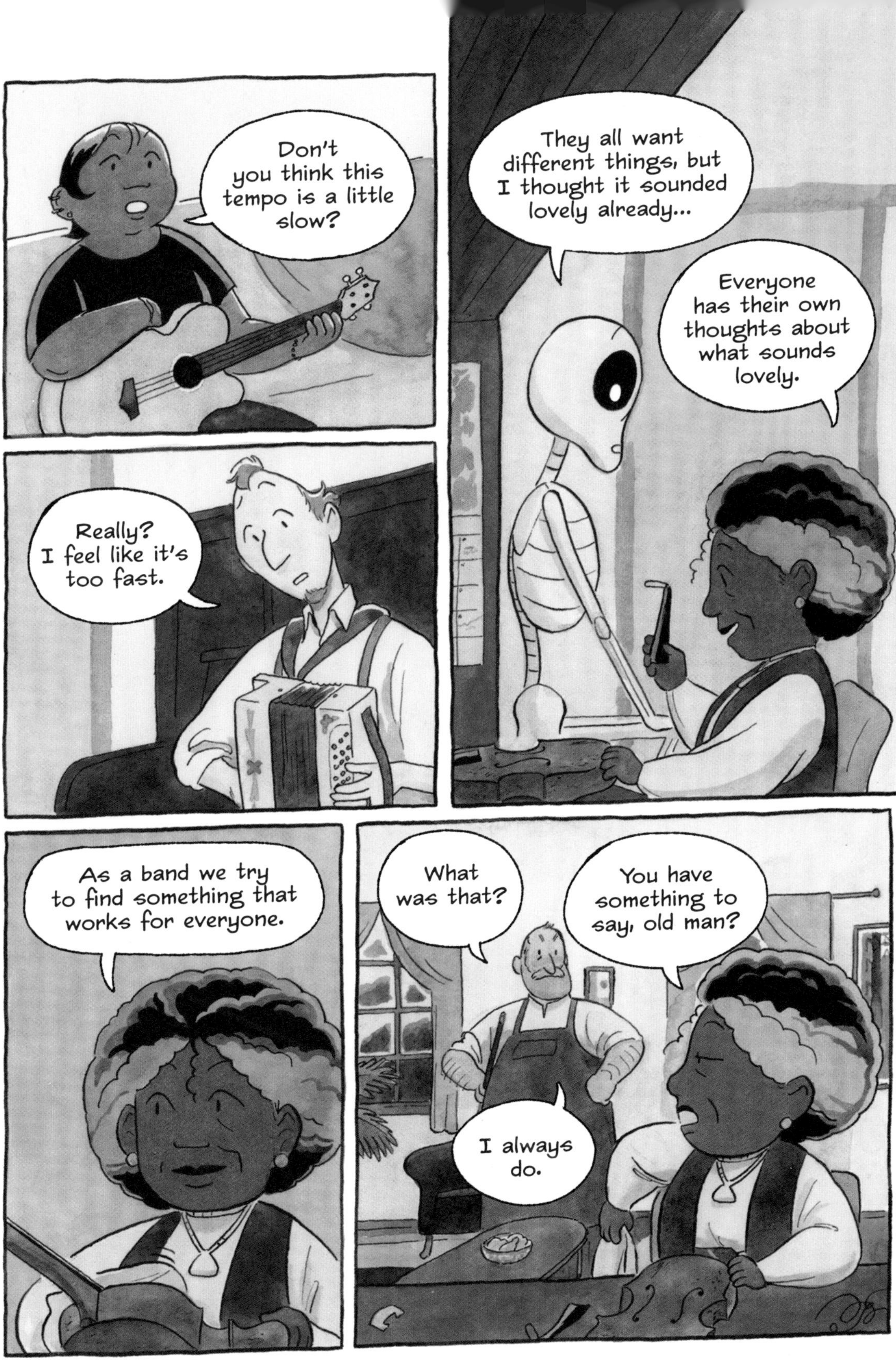
Don't you think this tempo is a little slow?
They all want different things, but I thought it sounded lovely already...
Everyone has their own thoughts about what sounds lovely.
Really? I feel like it's too fast.
As a band we try to find something that works for everyone.
What was that?
You have something to say, old man?
I always do.

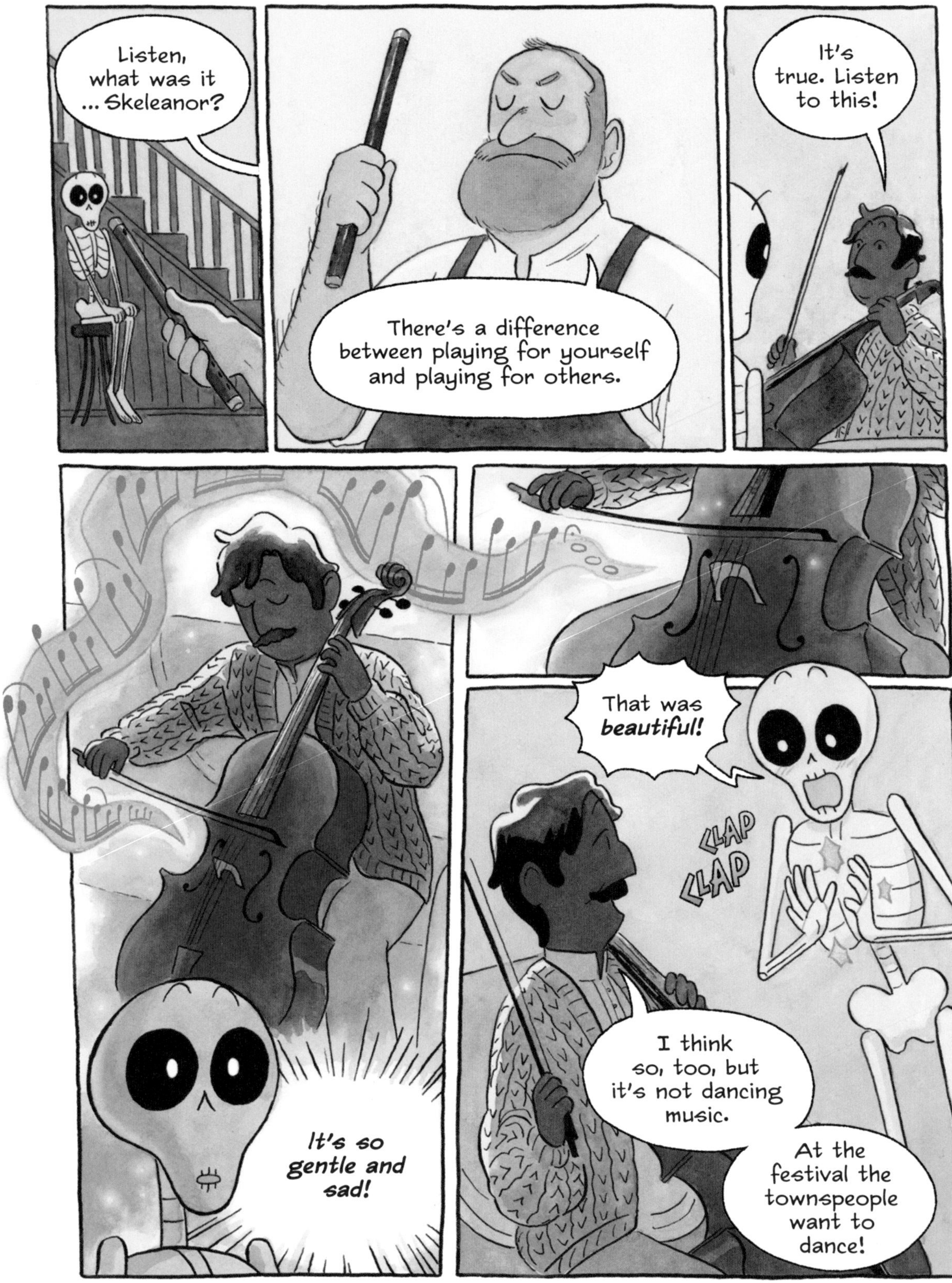
Listen, what was it ... Skeleanor?
There's a difference between playing for yourself and playing for others.
It's true. Listen to this!
It's so gentle and sad!
That was *beautiful!*
CLAP CLAP
I think so, too, but it's not dancing music.
At the festival the townspeople want to dance!

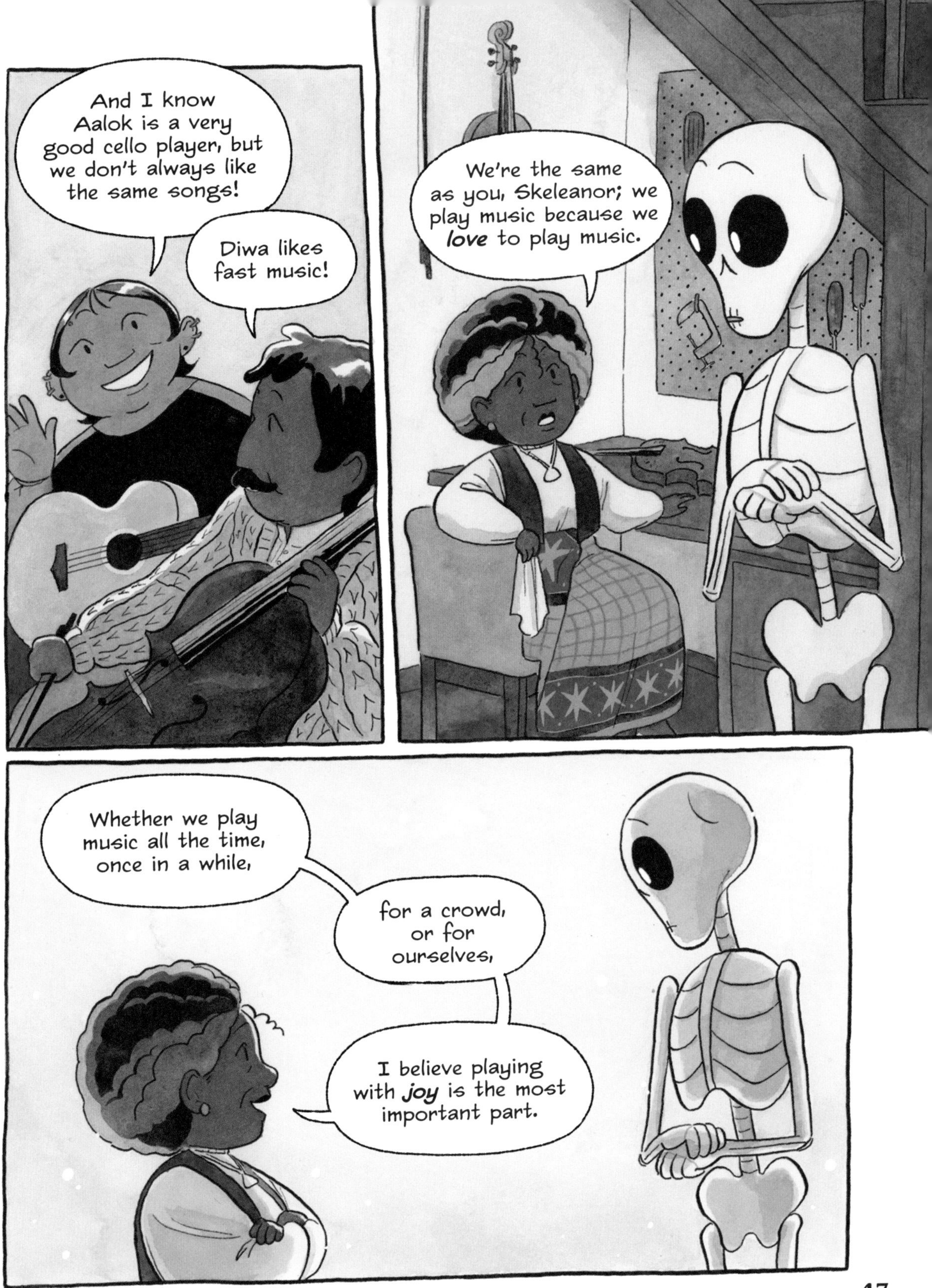
And I know Aalok is a very good cello player, but we don't always like the same songs!
Diwa likes fast music!
We're the same as you, Skeleanor; we play music because we *love* to play music.
Whether we play music all the time, once in a while,
for a crowd, or for ourselves,
I believe playing with *joy* is the most important part.

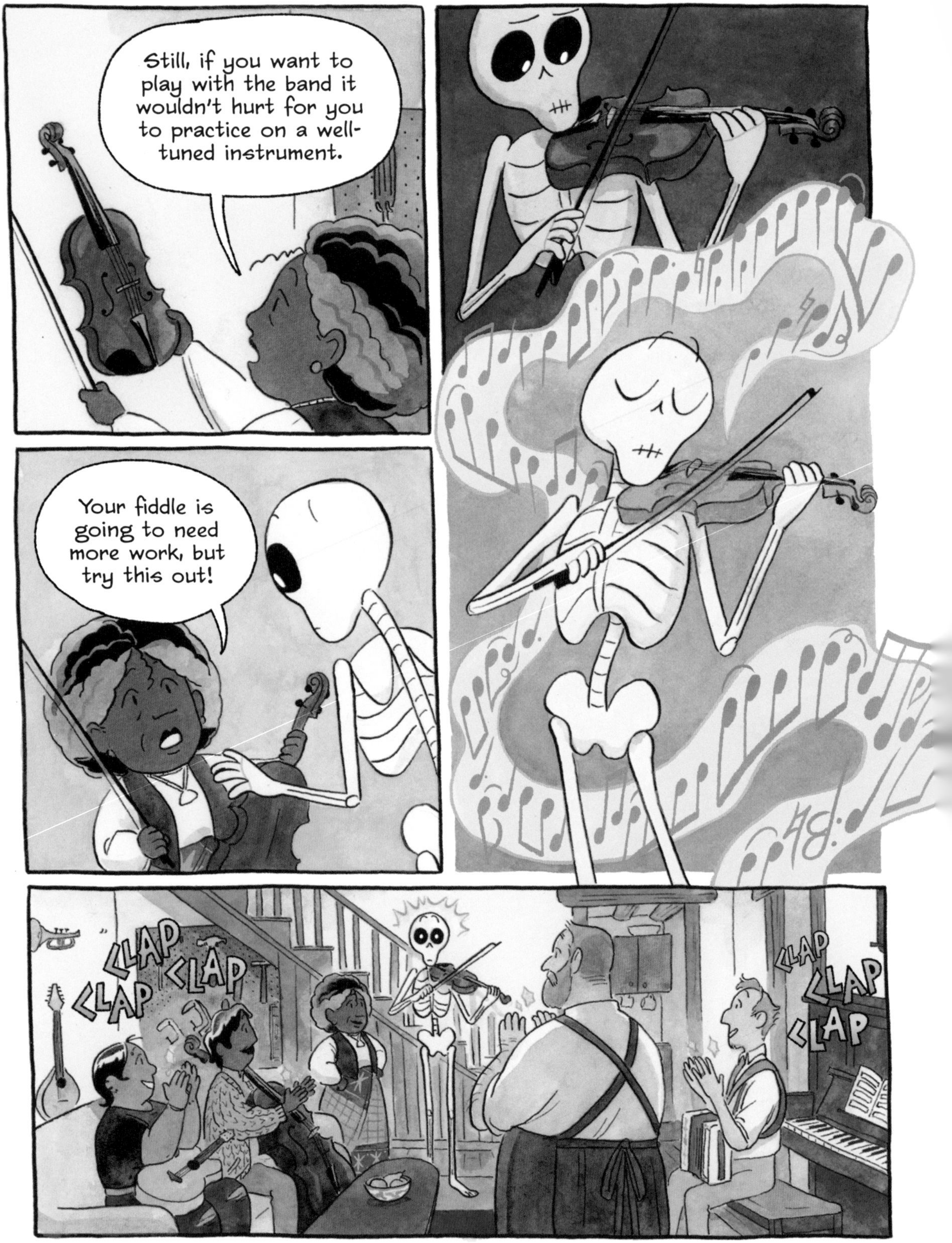
Still, if you want to play with the band it wouldn't hurt for you to practice on a well-tuned instrument.
Your fiddle is going to need more work, but try this out!
CLAP CLAP CLAP
CLAP CLAP CLAP

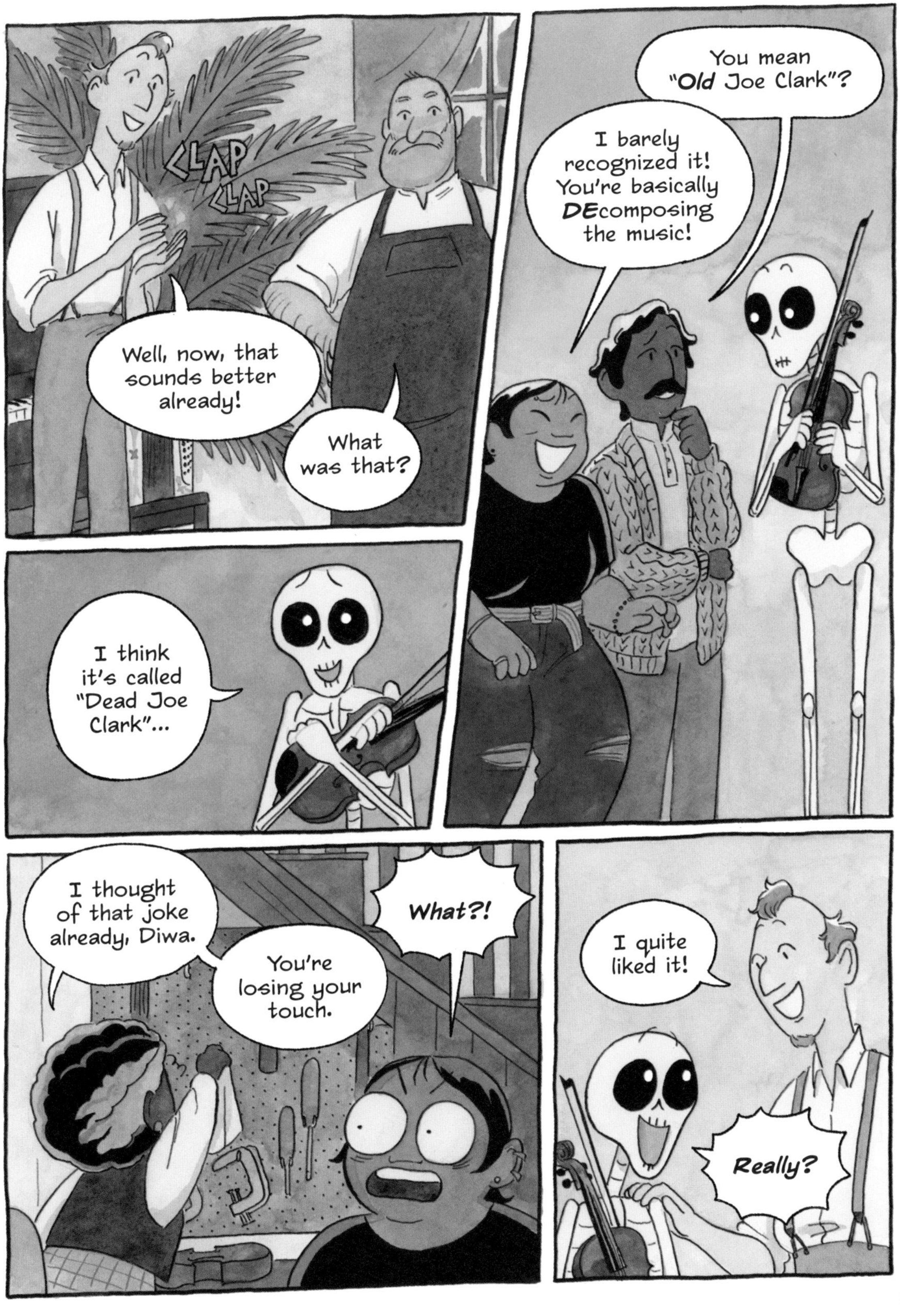
CLAP
CLAP
Well, now, that sounds better already!
What was that?
You mean "Old Joe Clark"?
I barely recognized it! You're basically DEcomposing the music!
I think it's called "Dead Joe Clark"...
I thought of that joke already, Diwa.
You're losing your touch.
What?!
I quite liked it!
Really?

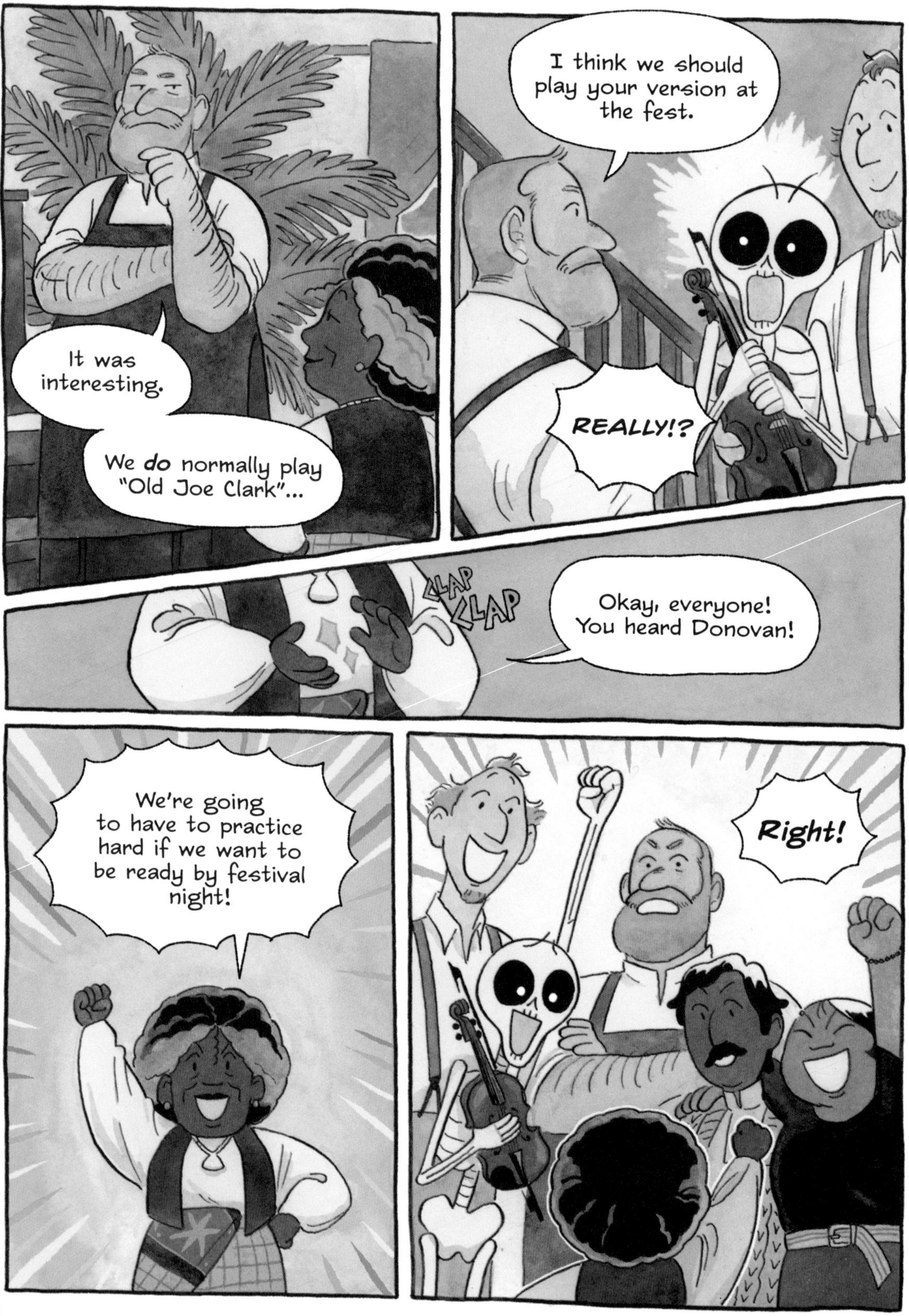
It was interesting.
We do normally play "Old Joe Clark"...
I think we should play your version at the fest.
REALLY!?
CLAP CLAP
Okay, everyone! You heard Donovan!
We're going to have to practice hard if we want to be ready by festival night!
Right!

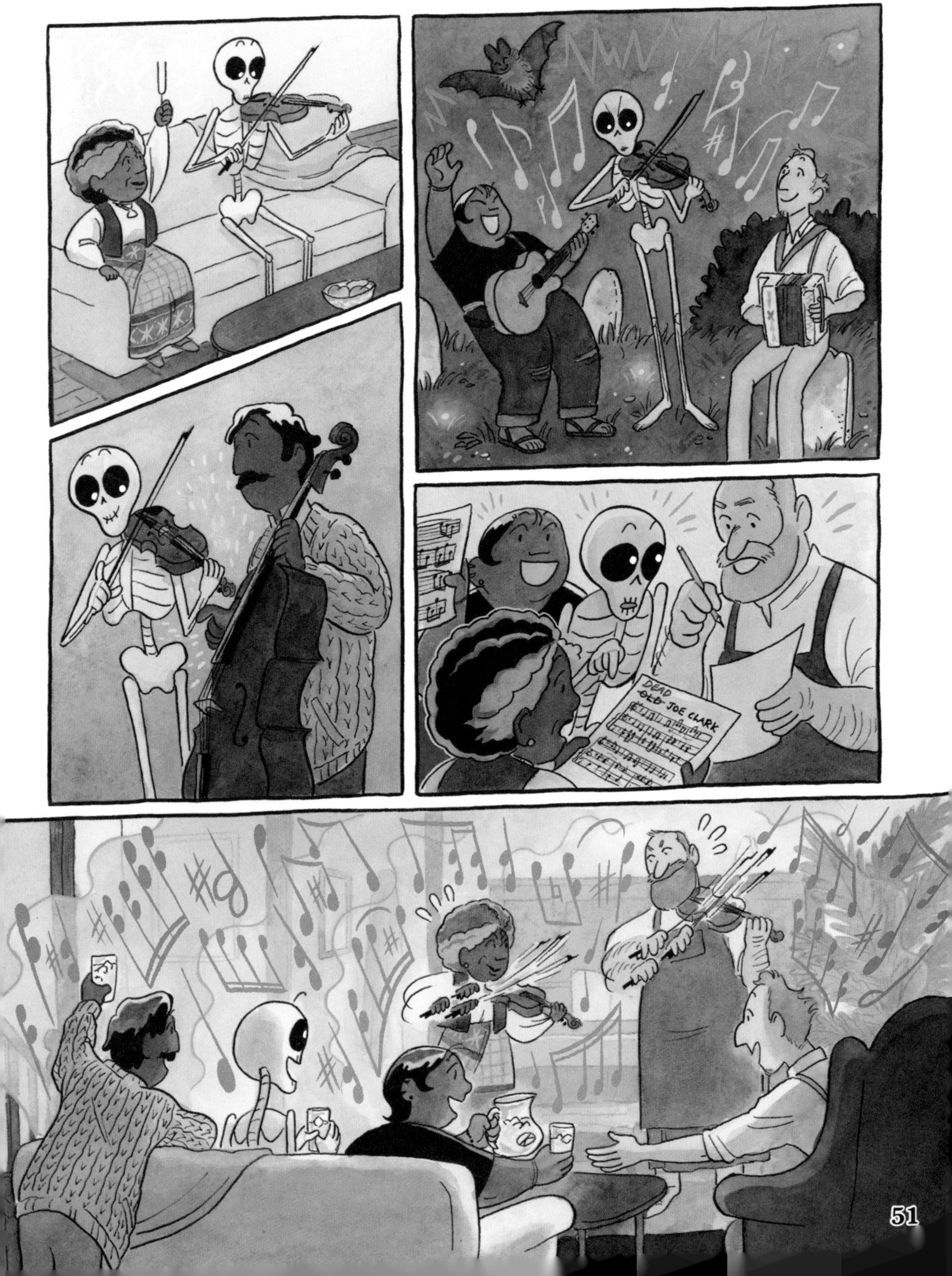
DEAD
~~OLD~~ JOE CLARK

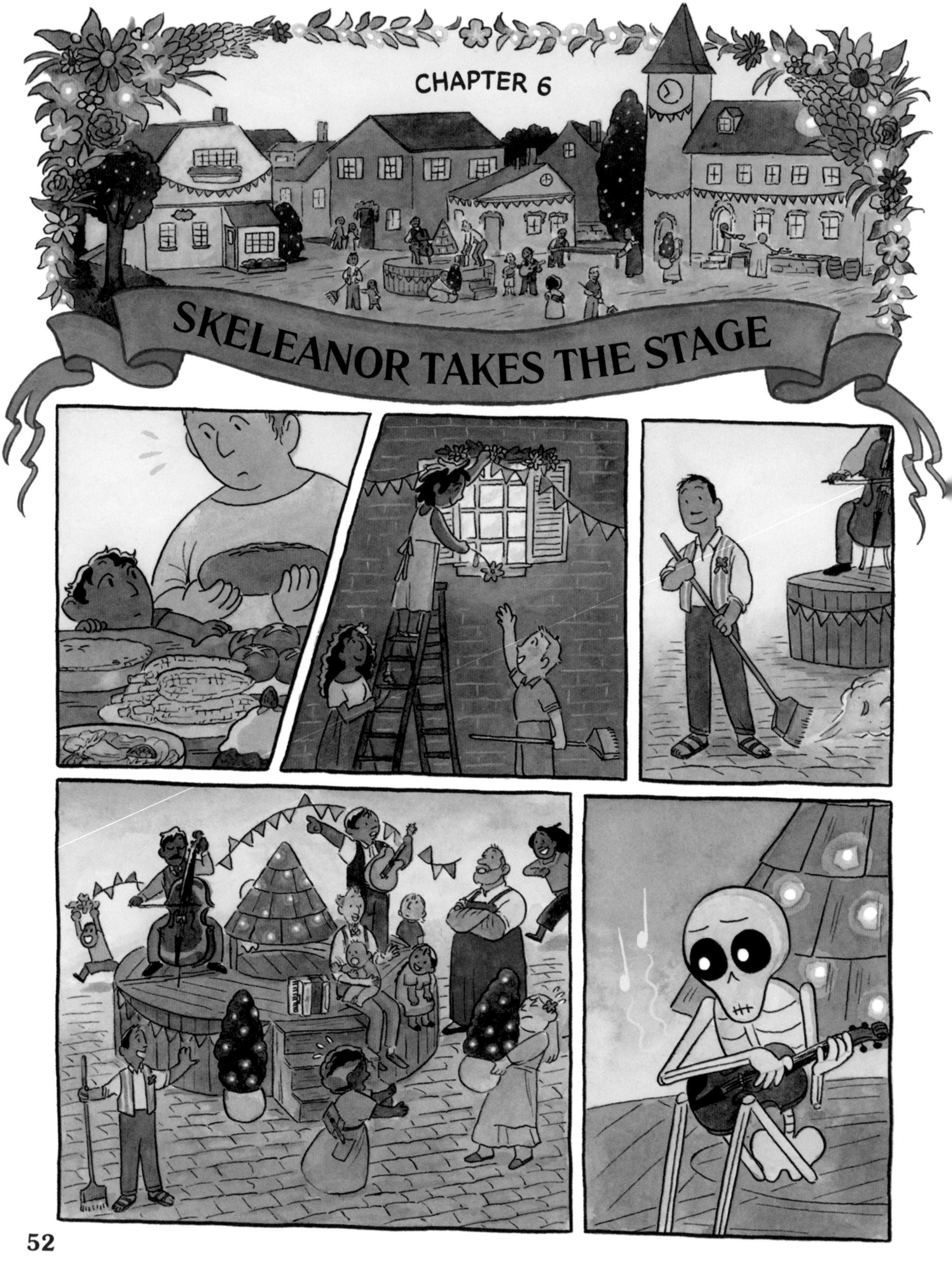
CHAPTER 6
SKELEANOR TAKES THE STAGE

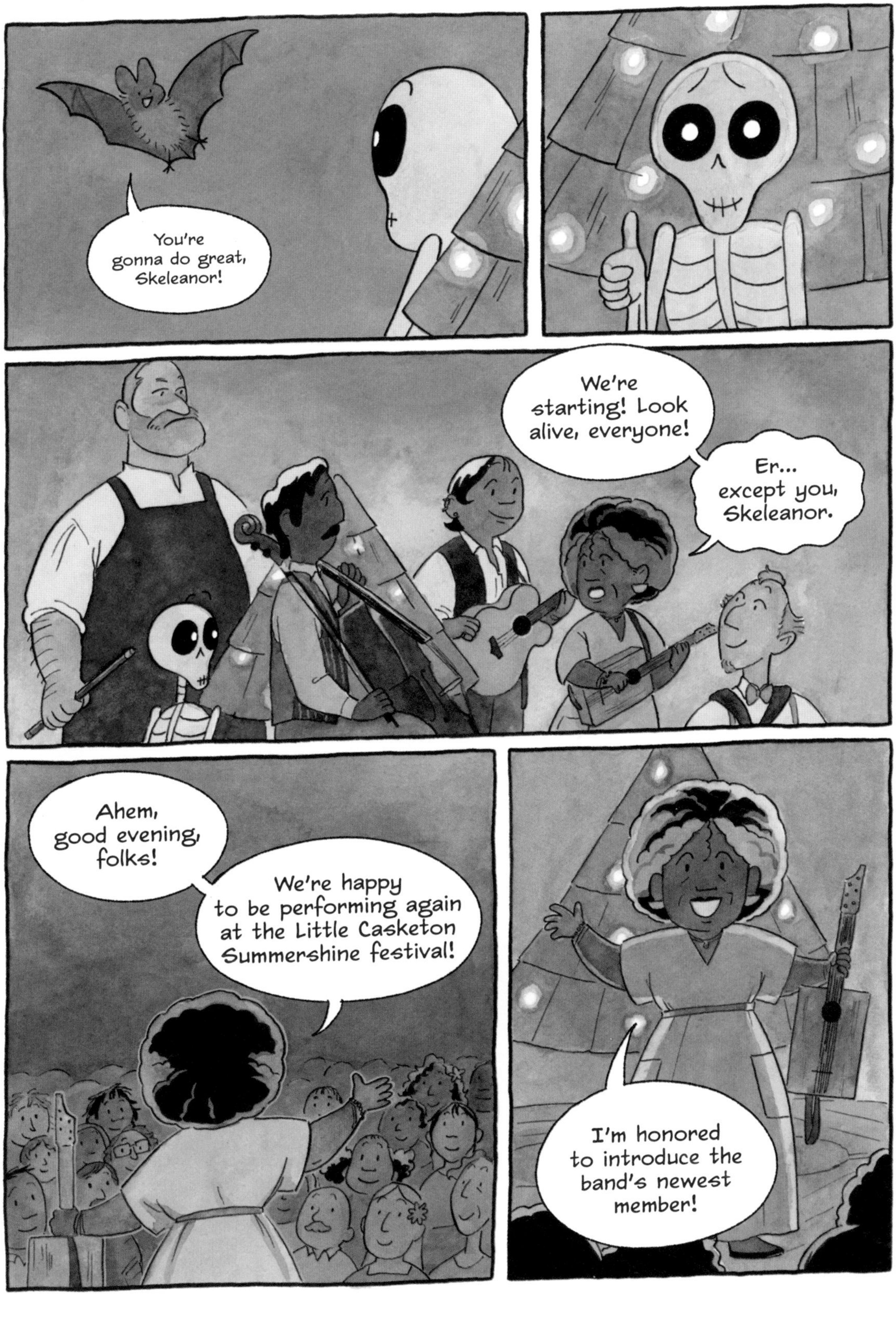
You're gonna do great, Skeleanor!
We're starting! Look alive, everyone!
Er... except you, Skeleanor.
Ahem, good evening, folks!
We're happy to be performing again at the Little Casketon Summershine festival!
I'm honored to introduce the band's newest member!

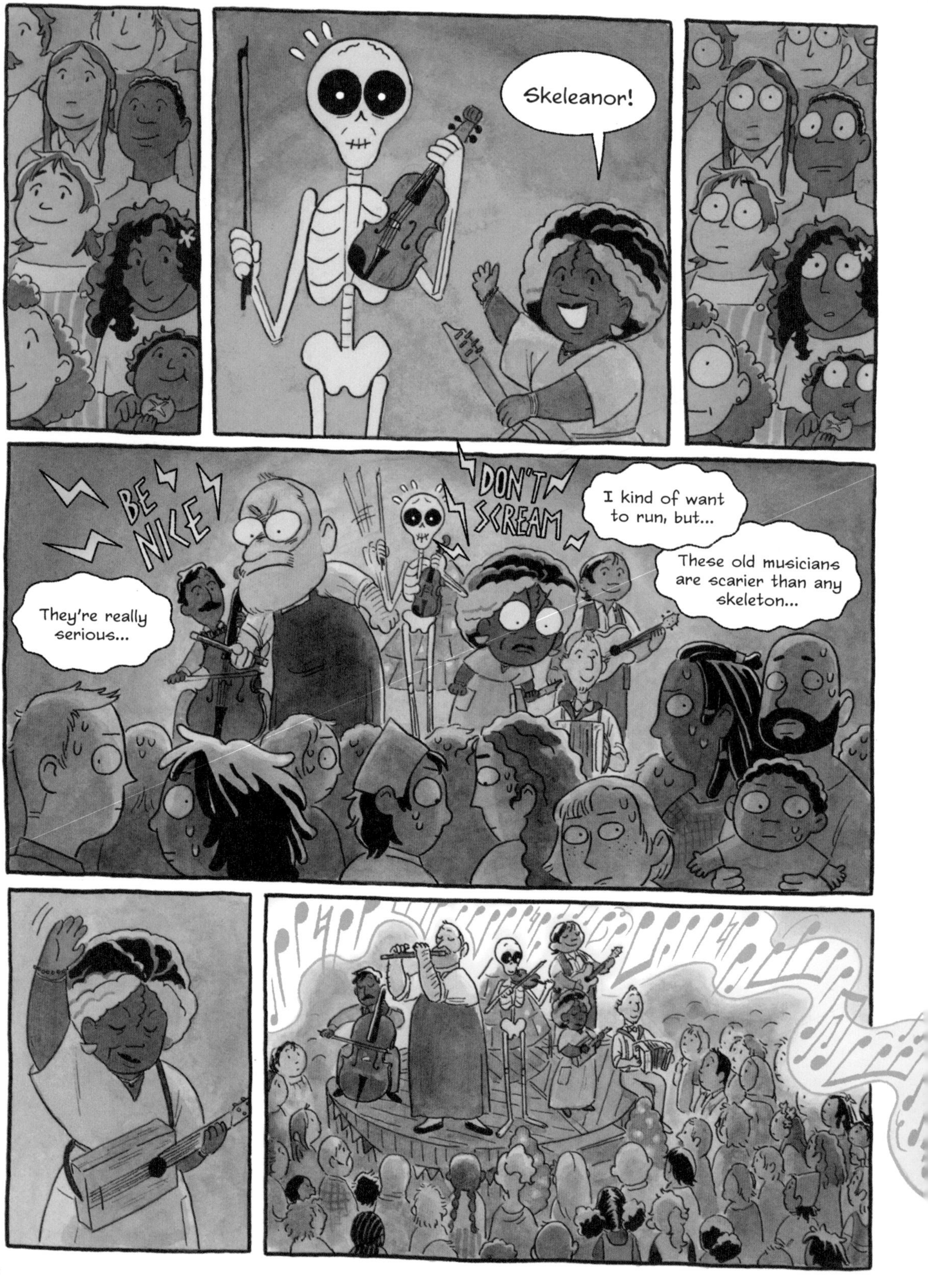
Skeleanor!
BE NICE
DON'T SCREAM
I kind of want to run, but...
These old musicians are scarier than any skeleton...
They're really serious...

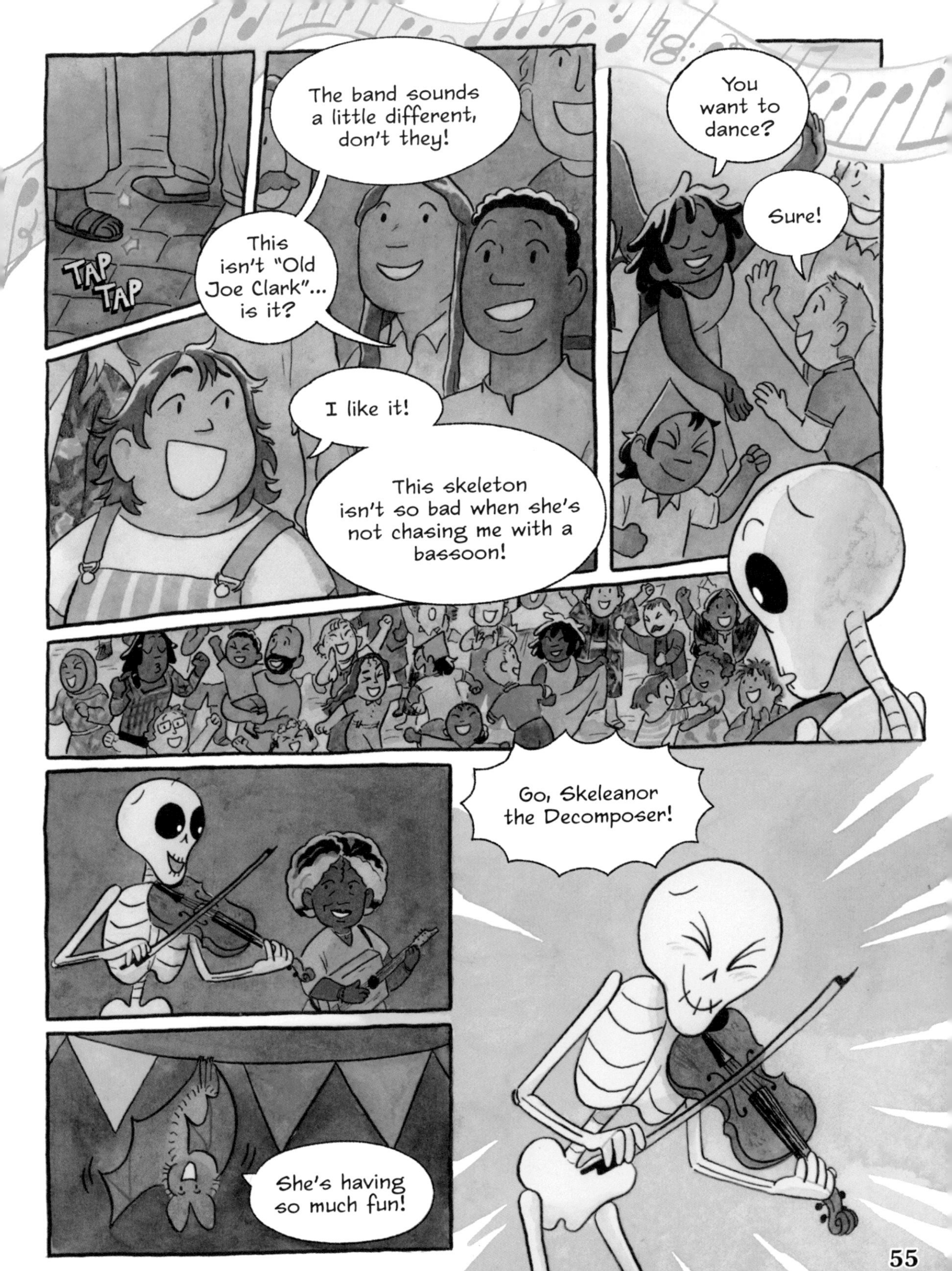
TAP TAP
The band sounds a little different, don't they!
This isn't "Old Joe Clark"... is it?
I like it!
This skeleton isn't so bad when she's not chasing me with a bassoon!
You want to dance?
Sure!
Go, Skeleanor the Decomposer!
She's having so much fun!

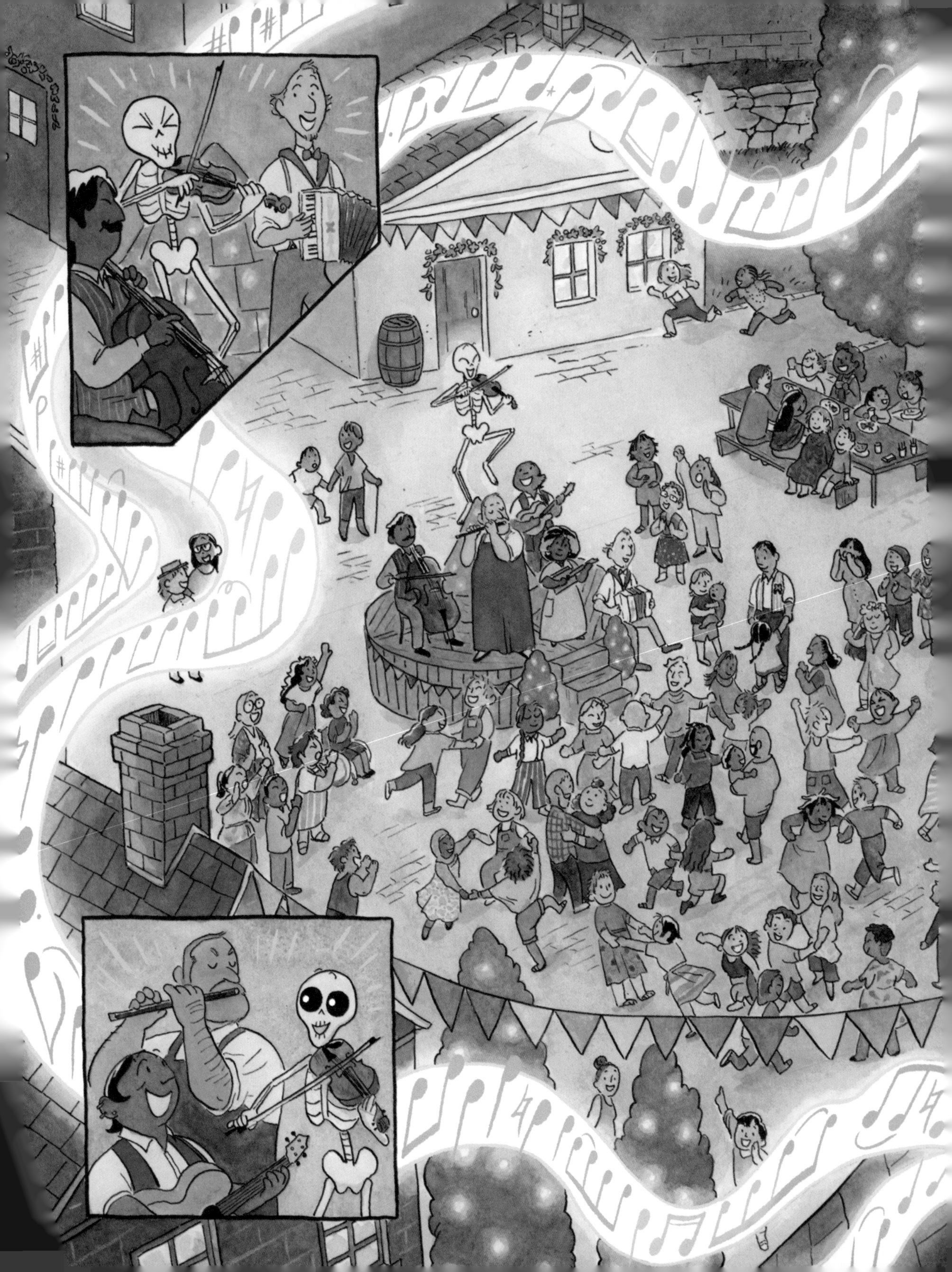

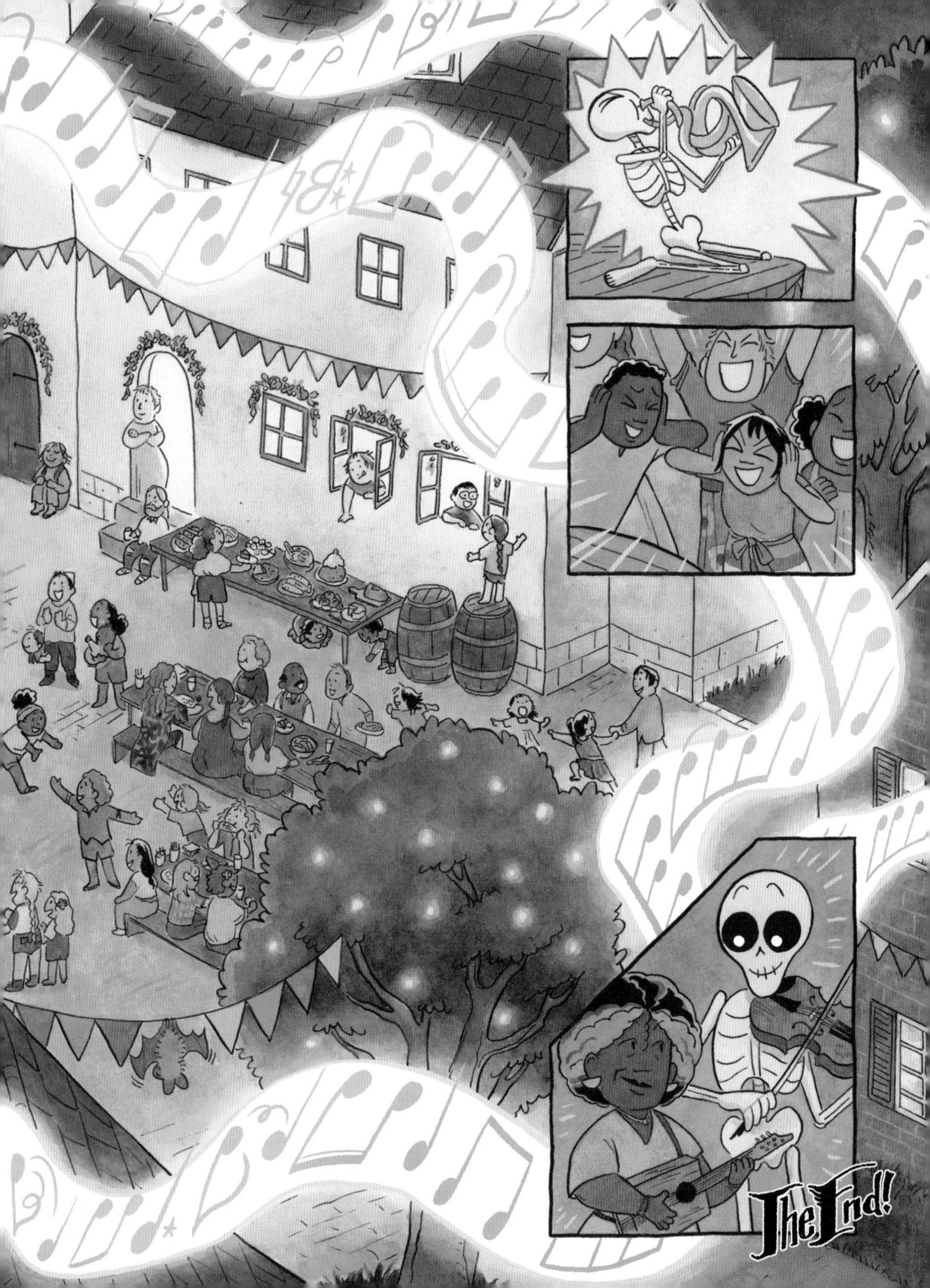
The End!

GLOSSARY

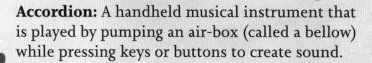

Accordion: A handheld musical instrument that is played by pumping an air-box (called a bellow) while pressing keys or buttons to create sound.

Bass guitar: The deepest-sounding instrument in the guitar family. Diwa plays it because she thinks it makes her look cool.

Cello: A large string instrument with a deep sound. It's very good for the kind of sad and romantic music Aalok likes.

Fiddle: A small and high-sounding string instrument. This instrument is called a violin when used for formal classical music and a fiddle for more casual settings (like a small-town festival).

Fife: A small woodwind instrument similar to a recorder or a piccolo.

Kabosy: A box-shaped guitar often heard in the traditional music of Madagascar. It's typically made by hand. Ms. Ratsimiziva made hers by hand, too!

Organ: The organ in this book is called a pump organ, and it works a lot like an accordion. The player uses foot pedals to pump air through the instrument.

Pluck: One way to play string instruments is to pluck the strings with your fingers instead of bowing them with a bow.

Rondalla: A band of string instruments played with a pick. The rondalla originated in Spain and is popular in Hispanic America and the Philippines. In different countries, a rondalla is made up of different instruments. Some rondallas do indeed contain a cello.